RIDE THE WILD TRAIL

Steve Santee came home to Powderhorn Basin with a fortune in gold. He planned to buy back his dead father's honor. But the law wanted Santee for train robbery. Nick Latzo and his gun-slingers wanted to murder Santee because he knew too much. And the Vigilantes wanted to give him a shotgun trial under the hanging tree.

RIDE THE WILD TRAIL

Cliff Farrell

GUNSMOKE

First published in the UK by Ward Lock

This hardback edition 2005
by BBC Audiobooks Ltd
by arrangement with
Golden West Literary Agency

ISBN 1 4056 8039 3

British Library Cataloguing in Publication Data available.

Printed and bound in Great Britain by
Antony Rowe Ltd., Chippenham, Wiltshire

RIDE THE WILD TRAIL

Chapter One

Along with a handful of other passengers, Steve Santee alighted from the westbound transcontinental express at Junction Bend to await the local which would carry him up the branch line to Bugle in the Powderhorn country.

He stood on the plank platform as the train proceeded on its way. He was nearly home. He pulled the thin, dry air of the plains deep into his lungs. To him, after nearly three years in the humid tropics, it had the sparkle and lift of champagne. He drank deep of it.

Ike Jenkins, the station agent, was puttering with the baggage truck. He was a spare, bony man with a penetrating voice. "You got nigh onto thirty minutes before the northbound local is due, folks," he informed the arrivals. "Time to wash the dust out of your throats an' eat a bite. There's establishments for both purposes right acrost the way, as you can see."

He added conversationally, "That train for Bugle is likely to be a mite crowded an' quite a bit lively. Cattlemen from the Powderhorn Pool are aboard, accordin' to what the telegraph operator tells me, an' they'll be jinglin' their spurs, an' maybe a little likkered up. They're on their way home from the Stock Association meetin' at Cheyenne, an' also from sellin' the Pool's beef gather. They hit the market top."

"What's the Powderhorn Pool, friend?" a bystander asked. "Sounds like something you fish in. And what's the market top?"

Ike Jenkins snorted at such ignorance. "I can see that you're a stranger in cattle country, mister," he said. "A pool is a bunch of ranchers who join together to round up an' sell their beef for the sake of easier handlin'. Market top means they got a durned good price for their cattle. An' about time too. They've had tough pickin's the last three, four years, what with blizzards an' robbery. They've got a right to stand

1

up on their hind laigs an' howl. I hear they'll be splittin' up more'n eighty thousand dollars when they git back to Bugle. That'll——"

For the first time Jenkins' eyes rested on Steve. His voice died off. He stood peering. "Steve Santee!" he said, and there was a curious mixture of surprise, scorn, and avid curiosity in his manner.

"You've got a good memory, Ike," Steve said.

"So has other folks in this country," Jenkins said. " 'Specially up around Bugle."

"And your tongue is still set on a loose pivot," Steve said.

Jenkins backed away from the impact of Steve's dark eyes and busied himself spotting the baggage truck against the wall of the station. He dropped his voice, but made sure it still reached. "That local might turn out to be plenty more crowded than I figgered," he informed bystanders. "Amos Whipple, himself, is aboard most likely. He's the big cog in the Powderhorn Pool. An' he ain't the forgivin' kind."

"What's he got to forgive, friend?" someone asked.

"The thievery of ten thousand dollars," Jenkins said. "That an' bein' double-crossed by a man he had trusted."

"I don't follow you," the bystander said. "Who——?"

But Jenkins, with a smirking sidewise glance at Steve, retreated into the station to avoid answering further questions.

Steve walked to the far end of the platform where he could gaze northward. Before him lay the great land, and all of it was as much a part of his life as yesterday. Here a man could see mile upon mile, mile upon mile. There was no end to it. There were no green jungle walls to shut him in. Only people like Ike Jenkins.

It was early September. The spice of sagebrush rode the breeze. It was a warm breeze, and yet it carried the promise of fall in its touch. The Mormon Buttes, flat-topped, their flanks banded in patterns of buff and lavender, rose to the north. Antelope country.

Beyond them, far away, a deep mauve shadow lay on the skyline. This might have been a line of clouds. It was, in fact, the massive bulk of the Powderhorn Mountains more than a hundred miles distant, the crests of which peered over the rim of the plains.

Steve gazed at that shadow. He laughed with the quiet joy of a man who had found something he had never ex-

2

pected to see again. "Hello, you rough heads!" he said to those mountains.

Crowding him were memories that eased some of the tautness in him. He was twenty-five and looked older. He was tall and needed meat on his bones. He had fought malaria and yellow jack and jungle rot in the gold fields of Nicaragua and Honduras and had gone into battle in bloody revolutions. He was thin and sallow, but this was already beginning to fade. He had put on a few pounds since setting foot again in the States.

He wore a dark store suit which he had bought four days previously in New Orleans. In his war sack was other new garb that he had acquired in Kansas City. His feet were in soft-topped cowboots, a luxury he had not known in a long time. He had very dark thick hair and straight dark brows.

He was thinking of rushing mountain streams in the Powderhorns and of battles won and lost with fighting trout. He was remembering the savor of elk steaks and venison, cooked over open campfires. And of frosty mornings in the high country, and of the slap of a beaver's tail on a clear green pool on hot summer evenings.

He felt that he was returning to the joy of living.

He turned and discovered that Ike Jenkins was watching him, that malicious glint brighter in his eyes. He saw the same look in other bystanders before they quickly averted their gaze. They had been talking to Jenkins and he had told them the story.

That clouded the day. Steve left his canvas luggage sack on the baggage truck and walked across the dusty street to an eating house. He ordered food and lingered over it, and over the coffee.

The smoke of the approaching local became visible and the wail of its whistle drifted across the flats. He paid his bill, returned to the station, and retrieved his luggage.

The clatter of the arriving train drowned out even Ike Jenkins' shrill voice. The engine ground past Steve, carrying its aura of steamy heat. It was followed by a yellow-painted combination express and baggage car and two wooden day coaches. At the rear were three freight cars and a gondola loaded with heavy mining machinery.

The windows in the coaches were open and heads emerged. The majority of the faces were the weathered countenances of men who had spent the biggest parts of their lives in the outdoors. They were Powderhorn ranchers and riders and they were noisy and waving bottles.

"Forty-two dollars an' four bits a head!" one yelled. "Highest danged price in years fer range cattle. I'm buyin' the wife a red silk dress an' a cast iron cookstove tomorrow, an' payin' off the mortgage."

Steve recognized the majority of them. Their activities had been a part of the range life he had known from childhood, for Powderhorn Basin was occupied by small ranches, some of which counted their cattle only by the scores. The two largest outfits in the Pool ran little more than a thousand head each.

He saw that some of them had also identified him. The word ran through the two coaches. There was a rib nudging and muttered comment. A touch of frost subdued their high spirits.

Steve gazed back at them. Luck had played an ironical trick on him by forcing him to face them like this, so unexpectedly. It would be easy to back off, avoid the issue at this moment, and wait for another train to Bugle on another day. In that way he could meet them on ground more of his own choosing.

He refused to damage his pride to that extent. He singled out two men with whom he had been well acquainted and friendly in the past. "Hello, Tim," he said. "Howdy, Race."

One answered confusedly, "Howdy." The other was too uncertain of himself even to frame a reply.

Both pulled back from the windows like startled turtles and seemed to be looking to someone else inside the coach for guidance as to how they should meet this situation.

Steve turned his back on them and watched two armed express employees emerge from the office in the depot bearing between them a padlocked, steel treasure box. The door of the express car opened and the box was shoved inside and signed for by a messenger whose cap bore the name of Northern Express. The responsibility for the treasure was now in the hands of the smaller, independent express company.

Some thirteen thousand dollars in gold coin which had cost Steve more than two years of toil and privation and danger was among the contents of that box. It all belonged

4

to him at the moment, but soon he would have only three thousand dollars to show for his efforts. The bulk of the money, ten thousand dollars, was the price he was paying as balm for his pride.

The gold had been mainly in raw dust, along with some Spanish coin when he had landed at New Orleans, but he had exchanged it for United States gold coin at the mint. Because of its weight he had entrusted the money to the express company when he had entrained for the cattle country.

When he had named Bugle as his destination, the clerk in the New Orleans office of Wells Fargo had frowned a trifle and had consulted his rate book. "We can carry your specie at the customary rates only as far as Cheyenne, my friend. Up to that point we carry gold for the same fee as iced lobsters and fresh eggs. Beyond that point, as far as the Utah line, the fee will be considerably higher. This also includes the territory northward to the Montana line served by Northern Express."

"How come?" Steve had asked.

"Organized gangs of outlaws are operating in that region, according to the bulletins sent out by the company," the clerk had said. "In addition to other crimes there have been some train robberies. We sustained one loss of more than fifty thousand dollars in a holdup near Rock Springs on the main line of the Union Pacific some four months ago. And not long before that, Northern Express was robbed of about the same amount just north of Junction Bend, where you will change trains. Northern Express has the express franchise on the branch line northward into Bugle and Powderhorn Basin. Your destination seems to have become a very rough community in the past year or two."

"Rough?" Steve had questioned.

"And wild," the clerk had nodded. "Big silver and gold mining has started in the Powderhorn Mountains, and the town is described in company information as the possible headquarters of some of these road agents and train robbers. You are sending quite a sum of money to Bugle. Be careful. Being forewarned is forearmed."

This was the first intimation Steve had that Bugle might not be as peaceful as he remembered it. He had not known that big, deep-shaft mining was in progress in the Powderhorns.

It had sounded fantastic. It had been like standing in broad daylight and hearing a grown man talk seriously of goblins and spooks. Steve's memory of Bugle was a drowsy mountain town of some two score structures. Bugle, to him, meant the clang of the hammer on the anvil in Sid Wheeler's blacksmith shop, the musty, nostalgic aroma of potatoes and apples and sacked coffee beans in Ed Leffler's general store. Or the fascinating glitter of a new saddle on display in the window of Hans Weber's leather shop. There had been three saloons and a pool hall at the south end of Bozeman Street, and the First Methodist Church at the north end, and Nick Latzo's roadhouse at the river ford not far out of town for garish entertainment. Now he was being told that Bugle had changed into some kind of a Gomorrah.

It still sounded fantastic as he stood here in the clean sunshine at Junction Bend, watching the sliding doors on the express car roll shut. He heard the metallic creaking as the messenger inside thrust the locking bars into their sockets.

He had had no other choice than to entrust the gold money to express shipment. Its weight would have been a giveaway if he had attempted to keep it with him as personal baggage, and he would also have had the task of attempting to stand guard over it every minute through four days of train travel. So he had paid the additional charge for expressing the coin.

He lifted his war sack, slung it over his arm. It contained his personal effects and his shaving kit and spare clothing. And it also held a .45 Colt six-shooter and belt and holster and a box of shells. The holster had the shine of much wearing. He had wrapped the gun in soft linen cloth for protection from damage.

He walked across the platform to the steps of the first coach and climbed aboard. He was aware that every eye now was following him. He opened the squeaky door and stepped into the coach to face them.

Saddles were piled in the aisles and bedrolls were stuffed into the overhead baggage racks. Only about half a dozen seats were unoccupied. Of the nearly two score of passengers in the car, all but a handful were riders and owners, returning from delivering beef at the shipping pens.

Roundup was over, the beef gather had been successful. The owners in the Powderhorn Pool were going home with the biggest profit in the history of the organization. They had

6

been whooping it up. The smoke of good cigars hazed the car and they had been drinking bonded whiskey.

He saw this joviality fade out of them. They did not speak as they eyed him. They merely sat silent and watching. And waiting.

One face emerged above all others. It was the stern, lined countenance of a weather-tanned, powerfully featured cattleman with shaggy iron-gray hair and brows and a drooping gray mustache. Amos Whipple, owner of the Center Fire, which was the biggest and most prosperous outfit in the Pool, was also chairman of the ranchers' organization and herd leader in all matters of decision and policy-making.

Steve watched Amos Whipple's eyes grimly inspect him. After three years there still was no toleration in the older man. He was not the forgiving kind. He had come up from Texas in the early days with the longhorns, fought the Sioux and the blizzards and the loneliness to establish Center Fire in Powderhorn Basin.

He was a strong man who took pride in never having gone back on a promise to a friend or to an enemy. He had no patience with weakness or dishonesty. He would have been a hanging judge if he had sat on the bench.

He was smoking a cigar, but he had drunk sparingly, if at all. He believed in seeing to it that he always had his mental faculties fully in control.

He continued to stare at Steve. In his deep voice he spoke through the spreading silence. "So you've come back to Bugle after all, Santee? Do you think that is wise?"

"I always intended to come back," Steve said. "I never had any other thought."

"Flocking to the feast, along with the other vultures," Amos Whipple said harshly. "Where have you been? In prison?"

"Not the kind you're thinking of," Steve said. "Not one with iron bars."

"Apparently whatever it was, it wasn't strong enough," Whipple said. "At least you're here, and you're not a blasted bit welcome. My advice to you, Santee, is——"

"I'm not asking your advice, Amos," Steve said.

A third party intervened. Steve discovered that Amos's companion in the seat was a young woman. She had been hidden from his view by the bulk of men in the forward seats.

She laid a hand on Amos's arm. "Uncle Amos!" she remonstrated, a reproof in her voice that silenced him.

She looked at Steve. "Hello, Steve!" she said. "It's good to see you." She spoke so that her voice carried to everyone in the car.

Steve stood gazing at her. He kept staring. Her eyes, a fine shade of gray green, looked back at him. "You skunk!" she said, a catch in her voice. "You act as though you don't even know me."

She was a gorgeous person. She had a small, straight nose and a nice mouth with a soft underlip. Her hair was a warm coppery shade with golden highlights, and her cheekbones gave character to the slimness of her features. She wore a cool green blouse and a pleated skirt. Excitement had brought a pulsing glow into her. The heat had accented a scatter of small freckles on her forehead. She was tanned healthily. Her fingers, where they lay on her handbag in her lap, were slender, but strong and carefully tended.

"And why should I know you?" Steve asked, a trifle numbly. "I once knew a girl as thin as a bean pole, who rode and looked like a boy. Before that I knew a pig-tailed, freckled little imp with legs as reedy as pipestems. She had a patch in the seat of her britches and used to throw stones at me and Doug Whipple when we wouldn't let her go swimming with us in Canteen Creek, because none of us owned bathing suits."

"That is not the sort of thing to tell here before other people," the gray-eyed person sniffed. "It was not that way at all, and I was a mere child at the time. As for being as thin as a bean pole, you never were very observant in matters concerning me. I do not believe I have changed that much in a few years. But, at least, you apparently do recall me vaguely."

"I don't know you," Steve said. "I only knew a person who, when we were kids, was as hard to get rid of as the hives whenever we wanted to go fishing or hunting. She should have stayed at home playing with dolls."

"It was because I always caught more fish and could track a bull elk better than the both of you," she said. "And I could swim faster than either of you, and you didn't want to be humiliated by a mere girl. That was why you and Doug Whipple used to pull my pigtails and call me a sissy."

"Your fishing ability is only a matter of your own conceited opinion," Steve said. He found himself fighting a tightness in his throat.

"I could catch more trout then than either you or Doug Whipple," she said. "And I can do it now, as I will demonstrate at first opportunity, if the two of you have the sand to face the test, which I doubt."

She was extending a hand. Steve took it shakily. She was smiling at him, and he saw some of the same emotion in her that gripped him.

"Thanks!" he said huskily as he held that warm, slender hand in his own. "Thanks, Bricktop."

"So you do remember me after all?" Eileen Maddox said, trying to maintain the bantering manner—and failing.

She added, "Welcome home, Steve."

Chapter Two

Steve didn't dare speak. He released Eileen Maddox's hand and moved ahead. Amos Whipple sat silent and grim, his lips fixed in utter disapproval of her action.

The next seat was occupied only by a cowpuncher. It was the rearmost in the coach. Steve would have preferred greater distance between himself and Eileen Maddox at that moment, for he was still fighting that lump in his throat. But to have retreated into the second coach would have looked like he was backing away from Amos Whipple. He swung his possible sack onto the overhead rack and took the vacant place.

Eileen looked around and smiled at him again. She studied him for a moment and her smile faded. He decided that she was seeing the changes three years had brought in him and did not like what she saw. She turned away.

Amos Whipple continued to sit stiff-necked and icily angry, because she had dared to differ with him. The puncher arose hastily, stumbled over Steve's feet, and departed for the other coach to seek an atmosphere that was less strained.

Across the aisle a sharp-featured man with jet dark hair and sideburns and eyes to match was listlessly dealing blackjack to two companions who were in a facing seat. He had the well-barbered look of a gambler who was in funds. The other two were older and of rougher formation. They wore holster guns. Steve tabbed them as the type who might be gambling-house bouncers and trouble shooters. He glimpsed the strap of an armpit holster beneath the linen coat of the younger one.

They were using silver dollars as chips, and the play was not high enough, evidently, to interest the natty one in sideburns. He inspected Steve boldly and a trifle insolently, as though indifferent to whether offense might be taken. He had witnessed the way Steve had been received by the cattlemen and Amos Whipple. And also by Eileen Maddox. He was curious, and evidently did not have the answer. His interest in Eileen was even greater, but she pointedly ignored him.

The train got under way and the drab water tanks and freight sheds at Junction Bend slid past, echoing the rumble of the wheels. The cars picked up speed in open country.

Steve slid over to the window and stared out unseeingly at the land. Eileen's warm friendliness and her courage in publicly defying Amos Whipple had helped. It had helped enormously, but the truth was that the zest of his return to these familar scenes was lost.

He hadn't expected them to forget entirely, particularly Amos. But neither had he expected them to be so unyielding. What was it that Amos had said—"flocking to the feast with the other vultures"? What had that meant?

They still believed that he had helped his father vanish from the Powderhorn country with ten thousand dollars that had belonged to the Pool. Only Eileen, apparently, did not share that opinion.

She had addressed Amos as "Uncle" although they were not related. It was a title of respect. Eileen had lost her parents when she was a small child. They had been killed by a snowslide that had swept down off Long Ridge and trapped their top buggy as they were driving from town to their ranch during a winter's storm. Eileen had also been in the buggy, but she had been dug alive from the avalanche by Steve's father and mother, who had been traveling the trail that day.

Eileen had been an only child. Amos Whipple, who had been a long-time friend and neighbor of her parents, had been appointed her guardian. He and his wife had taken her to Center Fire and had raised her, along with their own son, Doug, who was four years older than she.

A veteran cowboy named Shorty Barnes had been placed in charge of Antler. When Eileen was sixteen she had preferred to return to Antler to live and had hired a widow as housekeeper. Antler's holdings, like the majority of the outfits in the Pool, were modest but sufficient to afford a comfortable living when all went well.

Steve kept gazing at Eileen disbelievingly. It did not seem possible that the freckled, peppery-tempered tomboy he and Doug Whipple had ordered around like a slave could have blossomed into such an alluring creature.

Steve's father, Buck Santee, had owned the small OK ranch on Canteen Creek, where he had shared open range with the Antler and with Amos Whipple's bigger Center Fire to the east. The only other outfit in that end of the basin had been the Rafter O, owned by a cowman named Dave Garland.

Eileen's parents had not been the only victims of the snowslide. Steve's own mother had died of pneumonia that winter, brought on by her exertions in helping save Eileen.

Those tragedies had occurred during a hard winter in the Powderhorn. A worse one was to come, but it did not strike until four years ago, when Steve had grown to manhood. During that season of relentless cold and storm Steve and his father had seen more than half of their flourishing OK brand perish in the deep drifts and frozen flats.

Amos Whipple and other ranchers had been hit equally as hard. Beef gather the following summer had brought only a return of ten thousand dollars to be apportioned among all the members of the Pool. But, meager as was the return, the money was desperately needed in the basin.

Buck Santee had been chairman of Powderhorn Pool, and that had been a thorn in the flesh of Amos Whipple, who felt that he was entitled to that honor. Just as Steve had always been ill at ease in Amos's presence, his father and the Center Fire owner had never seemed to look at things from the same viewpoint.

Buck Santee, before he married and settled down, had been a rolling stone. He had been a cavalryman, stage driver, a deputy marshal in tough frontier towns, a lookout and trouble shooter in gambling houses, and had dealt poker and faro professionally in plush, high-play establishments in Denver and other places as far away as El Paso.

He had never made a secret of such things. He was well-liked, and men who had known him in his colorful past also knew that he had a reputation for strict honesty. Therefore they had chosen him as head of the Pool in spite of Amos's misgivings.

The money for the beef gather that year had been paid in gold as usual at the Kansas City stockyards by the commission buyers and had been brought to Bugle by train, just as the proceeds were being transported at the present moment.

The proportional settlement to the individual ranchers, after all expenses were tabulated and deducted, was to have been made at the customary barbecue and dance at the Spanish Flat schoolhouse, which had been the scene of such activities since the formation of the Pool. Pool Day, in good years or bad, was a time of high fiesta in the basin.

Buck Santee and an assistant had left Bugle for the schoolhouse after dark, with the gold on the back of a packhorse. Arrival of the money was always the high point of the celebration, and after its division the ranchers and their women would dance until dawn.

Buck Santee's companion was a ranching friend named Henry Thane. Both men carried six-shooters. The presence of the gold was supposed to be a secret, but it was an open secret, for this same procedure had been followed for so many years that it was routine.

There had been no lawlessness in the Powderhorn during those years, lulling the basin into a sense of security. Even the habitués of Nick Latzo's bawdy roadhouse in the brush near the river ford did not attempt to mingle with the citizens of Bugle.

Nick Latzo was a bulky, black-jowled, cigar-chewing man, whose Silver Moon offered gambling in tinseled surroundings, the music of an orchestra, and feminine entertainment. The place was anathema to the women of the country and spoken of by them in scandalized whispers. Law officers hunting fugitives always made Latzo's Silver Moon a port of call, usually without result. The patrons of the roadhouse did not talk. Tinhorn gamblers and taciturn men of mysterious origin hung out there. But they had kept their place, evidently considering Latzo's as a refuge where they only wanted to live and let live.

Steve's father and Henry Thane had never arrived at the schoolhouse. Henry Thane's body was found at daylight, partly buried under leaves and pine needles not far off the trail. His horse was grazing nearby, still carrying his saddle. Thane had been shot in the back of the head at close range.

Buck Santee and his horse were missing, along with the ten thousand dollars. The trail of his mount was lost after a short distance, wiped out by passing ore freighters which had furrowed a rain-softened road for miles.

Weeks afterwards it was reported that Buck Santee had been seen in Denver and later in Abilene, his old haunts where he had once been a professional gambler. As time went on it was rumored that he had been in San Antonio and in El Paso.

Amos Whipple swore out a warrant for Buck Santee's arrest, charging him with murder and robbery. The loss of the money placed ranchers in the Pool in precarious condition, and restitution was demanded in the courts.

What cattle and range rights Steve's father had owned were seized and sold under legal judgement. Only the modest, log-built house and spread which stood on homesteaded land remained immune.

Steve had found himself at bay. Amos Whipple had made it plain that he believed Steve must have had a hand in helping his father vanish with the money. "Blood is thicker than water," the Center Fire owner had kept repeating.

Steve had tried to face it out. He had scanned, inch by inch, the route his father and Henry Thane had followed that night. He had gone over it day after day, week after week, until time and weather had buried all hope of turning up any information in that manner.

He had scoured the country. He believed, in spite of the stories that his father had been seen alive in other places, that Buck Santee had been murdered at the same time Henry Thane had been killed, and that the body had been hidden in order to cast blame upon a dead man.

However, the word that Buck Santee had been glimpsed in faraway regions continued to drift in. This hardened public opinion against Steve. It was whispered that Buck Santee was in Chihuahua in old Mexico. Everyone knew that a man who had been well acquainted with him had talked to him there. Next he was in Vera Cruz, dealing Spanish monte in a gambling house. After that he was reported as living in luxury in Panama. So the tales went. Steve had never been able to trace down the source of these reports. But they confirmed the general belief that Buck Santee was alive.

Steve's persistence in hunting murder evidence began to be resented. He was ridiculed and taunted and accused of trying to set up blind trails to protect his father. Twice he fought men with his fists. These affairs had only hardened their antagonism. He had been arrested on both occasions and fined for disturbing the peace. He had been assured that any further trouble would land him behind bars.

Then Steve himself disappeared. He padlocked the doors of the house on Canteen Creek, where he had been born, and rode out of the Powerhorn between sundown and dawn.

He left a letter in the Antler mailbox, along with keys to the padlocks. The letter was for Eileen. It read:

> *Eileen:*
> *I'm going away for a while. If my father is alive I'll find him. Either that or prove that he is dead. I'll bring back enough money to pay off the Pool for what it lost. Ask Doug to keep an eye on the house for me until I get back.*
>
> > *Steve*

And now, after three years, he was back. Eileen was gazing at him once more, and he sensed that she also was thinking of that message.

She arose suddenly. Amos Whipple tried to stop her, uttering an angry protest, but she pushed past him and seated herself alongside Steve. Amos got to his feet, stamped down the aisle, and entered the next car.

The blackjack dealer across the aisle paused a moment to watch Eileen admiringly. Then he eyed Steve with increasing speculation.

"I still have the note you left for me," Eileen said, the rumble of the train covering her voice. "Three years is a long time. Was your—your quest successful?"

"You might call it that," Steve said. "At least I've brought back the money to pay off the Pool."

"Money? How much?"

"Thirteen thousand dollars in all," he said.

"You—you have that much with you? Now?"

"It's up ahead in the express car," he said. "Ten thousand

of it goes to these men in the Pool. I believe you'll be entitled to a share of it too, Eileen. Your beef money was in with the others."

"I don't want that kind of money," she said. "Where in the world did you get it, Steve?"

"I made the biggest part of it shoveling placer sand into a long tom trough in Nicaragua," he said. "I shoveled half a mountain through the riffles. A year and a half of it. Fourteen hours a day. When the placer wore out, I earned the rest of it running guns to a ragged little army in one of the banana republics down there. I was on the winning side. For once, justice and liberty got the upper hand. I had to earn part of my pay using a carbine. Sometimes a Gatling gun. The pay there was mighty low for what you put into it, just like it had been on the placer bars."

"How did you ever find such terrible places?" she asked.

"Hunting my father—tracing down those stories of him being seen here and there. After I left the Powderhorn I went first to Denver. Nobody there had seen Buck Santee in many years. Sure, they remembered him. He used to deal there in a gambling house. A square shooter. Abilene, the same. San Antonio and El Paso. I went into Mexico. Chihuahua, Vera Cruz. They had never heard of Señor Buck Santee. Then to Panama. I worked my way as a deck hand on a ship. You've never imagined anything like Panama. You sweat even when it's raining torrents. Beachcombers and outcasts from all over the world, preying on each other."

He was silent for a time. "That was the end of the hunt for me," he said.

"The end?"

"I had traveled ten thousand miles trying to find a man who had never left Powderhorn Basin," he said. "I had eliminated any last possibility, as far as I was personally concerned, that my father was alive. I was certain beyond question that he had been killed that night along with Henry Thane. About that time there was a gold strike in Nicaragua. So I joined the rush."

He peered out at the buttes and the blue sky. "And now I'm home," he repeated.

"Do you really intend to give the Pool that money?" she asked.

"Yes. At the Spanish Flat schoolhouse, if it's still there. As soon as I can do it. When is Pool Day?"

15

"Tomorrow. And the schoolhouse is still there."

She studied him gravely. "That money would give you a new start at ranching," she said. "You know that."

"I've never looked on it as my money," he said. "Money's not yours unless you think of it that way. But I'll have three thousand dollars left over for myself. I'll buy cattle. Is the house still all right?"

She nodded. "I stopped by there only yesterday. It's ready to live in. The fact is, Doug has been staying there a lot and taking care of it."

He gazed at her and she shrugged. "Doug and his father still can't hit it off. Doug never goes near Center Fire, even to see his mother."

They sat silent for a time. The blackjack game ended across the aisle. The two hard-visaged men dozed in the heat of the afternoon.

The younger one riffled the cards and continued to eye Eileen with bold interest. "Hello, Miss Maddox," he spoke finally. "You know me, of course. I'm Louie Latzo. Nick's brother. I've seen you often in Bugle."

Eileen ignored him. Louie Latzo was annoyed. He started to speak again.

"The lady doesn't know you," Steve said. "Let it ride that way."

Latzo had been drinking. He glared at Steve challengingly. But his companions had awakened and one muttered a growl of warning. Latzo scowled, but subsided. He finally laughed loudly, said something to the two, and took a drink from a bottle. He yawned and stared through the window.

Steve quietly studied Louie Latzo with interest. After the disappearance of his father he had fallen into the habit of visiting Nick Latzo's roadhouse at the river ford. His patronage at the Silver Moon, he had known, was not welcome, even though the elder Latzo had always greeted him with loud and effusive warmth. Latzo had been fully aware that Steve's purpose in mingling with the shady patrons of his place had been in hope of seeing or hearing something that would give him a clue to the fate of his father.

Nothing had ever come of it. If Latzo had any inkling of what had happened to Buck Santee he had kept it carefully concealed back of the beetling smile with which he greeted all outsiders and unidentified visitors who showed up

16

at the roadhouse. There had been no younger brother of Latzo around at that time.

Eileen guessed the trend of his thoughts and supplied information. "It didn't occur to me that you had never before seen Louie. He's an addition to our population since you went away. Unwanted, I might say. He showed up not long after you had left."

"Where did he come from?" Steve asked.

"Who knows? A gopher hole, probably. He came to share his brother's prosperity. Nick is said to be very fond of him. He keeps Louie well supplied with money, of which Nick always seems to have plenty. The Silver Moon is bigger and wilder than ever, what with the mines booming, and even cattlemen making profits. At least, so I hear. I wouldn't know at first hand. It's no place for a lady. And the Blue Moon is doing well also."

"The Blue Moon?"

"Nick has opened a second gambling house right in town," she said. "The Blue Moon. So we now have both the Silver and the Blue Moon in our sky in Powderhorn Basin."

"What's Louie doing on this train?" he asked. "Is he a member of the cattle pool?"

Eileen laughed. "Hardly. Louie probably doesn't know which end of a cow the horns grow on. He and his pals got aboard at Cheyenne. I suppose they were down there on a spree during the Stock Association convention. Cheyenne was humming. Louie likes the high life. His big brother sends the other two along to help him out when he gets into trouble, which is frequently. Louie is what you might call a little louse."

Steve sat thinking. He had never stopped believing that Nick Latzo could shed considerable light on what he wanted to know. There must be some way the man could be made to talk.

Eileen was silent also. Without knowing exactly why, he was aware that she knew the trend his thoughts were taking. He remembered now that it had been this way with them even as youngsters. He had always been an open book for her to read.

"Nick Latzo," she said, "is a very powerful man now—and dangerous."

Chapter
Three

The sun was low in the sky and beating hotly through the car windows. The fluted walls of the Mormon Buttes appeared abreast as the engine labored up the grade toward the Powderhorn Divide.

Steve touched Eileen's arm and pointed. "Pronghorns!" he said delightedly. "I made a bet with myself that we'd sight some along here. Antelope always hang around the buttes at this season of year. There's a spring under the base of that bluff where the juniper grows thick. I bagged a fine head there one morning."

A dozen or more antelope were standing in the sagebrush near the track, every head at attention, watching the train. Apparently they had learned that such mechanical objects offered no particular danger.

"Nothing has changed," Steve said. "Not even the people. And certainly not Amos Whipple. He still sits in judgement on others."

"Perhaps you've changed," Eileen said.

"For the worse, you mean?"

She sorted through her mind for an answer. "I really don't know. You're grim, Steve. And much, much older than you should be. You look like—well like a man who doesn't give a hoot about the rights of other people if they happen to stand in his way."

"Nobody ever gave a damn about my rights," he said.

"Then you are bitter," she said. "You've come back with a chip on your shoulder. Next it'll be a gun at your side. You bear a grudge."

"That might be one way of putting it," he said. "If they want trouble I'll not back away from it this time."

"It isn't worth it," she said anxiously. "You owe yourself a chance to forget."

"I'll owe myself nothing, nor them either after I pay them the money they accuse my father of stealing," he said.

"But it isn't easy to forget bitterness. You can't rub out deeds with words, you know."

Across the aisle Louie Latzo was staring at the antelope. The train had now drawn abreast of the animals, which were less than fifty yards away.

The band wheeled suddenly to retreat. Even as the antelope began their first stiff-legged jump, Latzo snatched from his shoulder holster a silver-mounted six-shooter and began firing as fast as he could thumb the hammer.

The antelope were moving parallel with the laboring train, and even an average marksman would have registered at that short range. But Latzo was in a frenzy, as though fearing his quarry would escape. It was the passion to kill and kill, Steve realized.

The man spilled his shots in a shocking thunder of sound. Bullets kicked up dust around the running animals. Latzo was shooting into the band indiscriminately, trying to register hits on as many targets as possible.

Only one bullet found a mark. A young doe stumbled and went down. It arose bleating, then fell again. It had a bullet-broken leg.

The remainder of the band were off and bounding in frantic effort over the sagebrush. Latzo, laughing shrilly, snatched a six-shooter from the holster of one of his companions. He had emptied his own gun. He eared back the hammer, intending to send another hail of bullets among the fleeing animals.

Steve was out of the seat and past Eileen in a lunge. His hand caught the .45, his thumb jamming the hammer. He twisted the weapon from Latzo's grasp.

The doe was still hobbling along, trying to overtake its companions, its shattered front leg dragging grotesquely. Steve lifted the gun and fired twice. Luck was kind to him, for the distance had widened. The injured animal, which would have been a living prey for coyotes and magpies, reared, then went down with the limpness that was the mark of a death blow. At least one of the mercy shots had scored.

"Why, you . . . !" Latzo screeched in a rage.

He swung a punch at Steve's face. Steve, with his free hand, blocked that blow. Latzo tried to snatch the pistol from him. There was the savagery and rage of a humiliated small mind in the man's thin face. If he could have gotten possession of the loaded gun he would have killed.

But Steve shoved him roughly back into the seat and maintained possession of the weapon. Latzo's two companions had been unable to move until now because of the fast action and the close quarters. The one who still was armed saw his chance to attempt to draw.

"Stay out of this!" Steve said and backed off a pace, the captured .45 covering the three of them. The man went motionless. After a moment he carefully lifted his arms well away from his gun. He was coarse-featured, thick-lipped, with a nose that had suffered damage in the past. He said nothing, nor did his companion, who was shorter and blocky of shoulders, with muddy brown eyes and a small, sand-colored mustache.

Taut silence held the coach. Steve yanked the six-shooter from the holster worn by the thick-lipped man. He flipped open the chamber and spilled the live shells out the window. He did the same with the cartridges in the weapon he had appropriated. Louie Latzo's ornate pistol was empty. Steve lifted it from Latzo's holster.

He sent all three guns skidding down the floor of the aisle to the far end of the car. "Pick 'em up after you cool off," he said. "And not before. In case you have more shells in your pockets, don't reload as long as you're on this train."

He eyed Latzo. "After this," he went on, "if you want to kill game, pick your target and shoot it clean and honest. Don't wound animals just to abandon them in their misery."

Latzo and his companions glared around. No one had anything to say. The cattlemen were eying them stonily. Whatever other opinion they might hold in regard to Steve, it was evident that he had their grudging approval in this matter at least.

Latzo spoke in a choked, strained voice. "All right, mister. I'll remember you, whoever you are. I hope you won't be hard to find."

"My name is Santee," Steve said. "Steve Santee."

A flicker of surprise passed over Latzo's features. Evidently he had heard the story of Buck and Steve Santee.

"I'll be at my home on Canteen Creek if you want to look me up," Steve went on. "I'll also be in Bugle whenever I have a mind to come there. You won't have any trouble finding me."

He wasn't talking to Louie Latzo as much as he was addressing the men of the Powderhorn Pool.

"I'll find you," Latzo promised fervently. "You can bet your last slick nickel on that."

Steve sat down alongside Eileen again. She looked at him and said, "Thanks."

Some of the hard fury slacked out of him. He smiled at her. She leaned close. "Louie Latzo meant what he said about getting even," she said. "Watch out for him, Steve. That big ugly one goes by the name of Al Painter. The other one is called Chick Varney. They've both been in gun fights and brawls several times. They're vicious persons."

"How does a man go about watching for them?" he shrugged. "Usually that's another name for running away."

She sighed. "You haven't changed in one respect at least," she said. "You always were mule-headed about such things."

The train rolled on northward. Steve watched the Powderhorns take shape and rise until they filled the sky ahead. Some mountains, he reflected, were feminine in character. Soft and mysterious and beautiful and fascinating. The Powderhorns were ruggedly masculine. They were as wild and untamed as a great bull elk or as the grizzlies and the mountain sheep which ran free and above the world on their high flanks.

Eileen watched him. "The Powderhorns don't change either," she said. "You always looked at them as though you were looking at a friend—a very close friend. And that's the way you're looking at them now."

"They're honest," he said. "I understand them and they understand me. It's good to know them."

She sighed again a trifle impatiently and said nothing more. Amos Whipple returned from the rear car and took his place in the seat ahead. The set of his shoulders was evidence that Eileen was not forgiven for standing against him.

Sundown came. The Powderhorns began to draw purple shadows about their shoulders as twilight moved in. Bugle was little more than thirty miles away. Louie Latzo and his two pals sat sullen and forboding across the aisle. Their guns still lay untouched at the end of the car.

Many of the cattlemen were dozing now. Eileen had her eyes closed, but Steve knew she was not sleeping.

The train abruptly slowed and the whistle sounded. Men roused and crowded to the windows, shouting and pointing. Two riders were galloping alongside the tracks. One left the saddle and leaped agilely onto the steps of the coach. The other, who was a cowpuncher, swerved away, seized the reins of the riderless horse and pulled up, laughing and waving his hat.

The occupants of the car were delighted. They were cheering and guffawing. As the arrival entered the car they greeted him with friendly jibes and comment.

"Tryin' to avoid buyin' a ticket, huh, Burl?"

"You ought to try that stunt at the Frontier Days show, Burl. You'd shore win a prize—or a busted laig."

"I reckon it wasn't us boys you was so anxious to see, Burl," another said. "There must be some other attraction aboard this train."

Burl Talley was grinning and taking sips from bottles that were being pushed at him. "Sorry I couldn't make it to the convention at Cheyenne, boys," he said. "But I wanted to be in on part of the fun at least. Red Sealover and me rode all the way across the basin from the ranch today to meet this train."

Talley's glance searched the coach and rested on Eileen. Steve realized that she was the attraction the speaker had mentioned. Talley pushed past hands that tried to restrain him and moved down the aisle.

Steve knew him well. He was a straight, lithe, handsome man of forty who carried himself with poise and assurance. He had thinning, well-barbered brown hair and brown eyes that were bright and alert. He had come into the Powderhorn some ten years in the past on foot and in search of opportunity. He had swamped for freighters and had worked in lumber mills. Within a few years he owned a lumber mill of his own in Bugle. From there he had branched into other prosperous sidelines.

Talley now wore the garb of a cattleman. It was expensive regalia, but conservative.

Eileen must have guessed the trend of Steve's thoughts, for she explained. "Burl has gone into cattle also, since you went away, in addition to owning the planing mill and lumber yard. He took over the Rafter O in our end of the valley when Dave Garland had to sell. He's a member of the Pool."

Talley came striding toward Eileen and it occurred to Steve there was confidence in his smile and also something demanding, as though he was sure of himself, but felt that he was not receiving entirely all that was his right.

22

"You went to considerable trouble to join the crowd, Burl," she greeted him.

"Not the crowd," he corrected, taking her hand. "You. Again I want to say how much I regret that I couldn't go with you and the others. I just couldn't shake loose from several business snarls."

She laughed and slowly withdrew her hand. But she was not annoyed by his public display of affection. His intentions were plain enough. And though he was considerably older than she, he had much of the quality that would hold the feminine interest. Most any girl, Steve reflected, would consider Burl Talley quite a catch.

Talley had been so absorbed in Eileen that it was not until now that he really looked at Steve and recognized him. He straightened a trifle, and his mind must have flashed to some disturbing thought, for he frowned a little and stood as though trying to decide his course.

"Well," he said. "Santee! Steve Santee!"

"Hello, Burl," Steve said.

Talley did not offer his hand. He cleared his throat and said, "I believe it might be cooler in the other car, Eileen. Perhaps——"

"Steve and I have a lot to talk about," she said. "We grew up together, you know. Some folks called him and me and Doug Whipple the three little devils. Others had still stronger names for us."

Talley forced a strained smile. "Is that a fact? Perhaps you and I can talk later, my dear."

He shook hands with Amos Whipple, who shrugged helplessly. Talley gave Steve a concerned, measuring look, then walked on out of the car and into the other coach.

Steve did not speak for a time. "Burl Talley thinks you are not in very good company," he finally said.

"Does he?"

"You value his opinion, I take it?"

She turned a cool, slanting inspection upon him. "Why do you ask?"

"You're good at ducking straight answers," he said. "You like him, don't you?"

She frowned a little over that question as though it was a matter that must be examined. "I know of no reason why I should not," she said. "Burl's solid, substantial. And he doesn't try to pry into my private thoughts."

"I'll change the subject," Steve said. "I can see that your temper is beginning to simmer up. Next thing I know you'll be kicking me on the shins to put me in my place. Is that big rainbow lunker still in Black Rock pool, waiting for me to drift a bucktail fly into the riffle back of that boulder in the middle of the river where he hangs out?"

"He's still there," she said. "Along with a couple of his brothers who've grown up. I've saved them for you. I haven't fished Black Rock since—well, since you went away. I'm running Antler, now that I've grown up. Shorty Barnes is really the one who still does the running, but I'm learning. Between the two of us, Antler is doing well. The basin's luck changed the past few seasons. Mild winters, healthy calf crops, and plenty of grass. I've got nearly six thousand dollars coming out of the beef pool. I'm a full-fledged member of the Stock Association now. that's why I went along on this trip."

"How's Doug?" Steve asked. "Is he still rolling his spurs high, wide, and noisy, and kissing all the girls?"

Eileen hesitated a moment. "He's still trying to kiss all the girls at least," she finally said.

Steve believed he knew the reason for that pause. Amos Whipple had always hoped that his son and Eileen would marry. In fact nearly everyone in the Powderhorn had taken it for granted that she would wed Doug Whipple—provided she didn't marry Steve Santee. They had been so young that marriage was a subject that only elderly people thought about or talked about. Such a matter had been fantastic to them . . . then.

All three of them had been born in the basin. Steve and Doug Whipple had attended the Spanish Flat schoolhouse together and had hunted and fished and played and squabbled side by side.

Eileen had made herself an insistent participant in their activities in spite of the lofty scorn with which they looked down upon her from their more advanced masculine years.

It had been one of their responsibilities to see that she got safely to school and back each day on the ancient, plodding saddle stock that all three of them were compelled to ride for the sake of her tender years.

That had been very humiliating to Steve and Doug, and had brought down on them the derision of more fortunate ranch youths who were permitted to ride spirited horseflesh. Many times they had stood back to back against odds, defending their honor with their fists. And Eileen had joined with them frequently, fighting like a wildcat against their opponents.

Beyond that, Steve and Doug Whipple, when away from the dampening influence of a girl's presence, had been reckless, hell-for-leather striplings who were the prank-playing terrors of the range.

It was Steve who had been the balance wheel, the one who had kept the mischief-making within the bounds of boyish high spirits. For, in Doug, there had been a moody, heedless thirst for excitement and high experience and a disregard for the rights of others.

Doug and his father had always been at odds, and he had felt the iron hand of Amos Whipple's unswerving discipline many times. This had driven them farther apart until Doug, when he was nearing manhood, had left Center Fire, vowing that he would never again bow to his father's will.

Steve and Doug had also drifted apart as they reached maturity. More and more they lacked mutual interest. Doug began putting in his time traveling with flashy, hard-drinking cowboys.

But the affection that had been welded between them in boyhood was as strong as ever. Steve believed he knew more about Doug Whipple, and understood him better, than any man living. He knew Doug's weaknesses and irresponsibility and knew his strength. On one occasion Doug had saved his life.

"If Doug's gone and caught that big walloper at Black Rock I'll wring his neck," he said. "He knows that's my fish. He's got his own fishing hole just above that spot."

"I'm afraid the only fishing Doug does nowdays," Eileen said reluctantly, "is from a whiskey bottle."

"So that's how it is?" Steve said.

"He and Uncle Amos never came to an understanding," she said. "They're farther apart than ever. Doug doesn't seem to have any purpose in life, unless you call drinking and having a wild time a purpose. Maybe you can talk to him."

"I never was able to do much with him in the past," Steve shrugged.

"If you can't, then no one can," she said. "Doug thinks a lot of you, Steve. He talks about you every time we meet."

"What's he doing, outside of the things you mentioned?"

"He rides for one outfit or another," Eileen said. "He

worked roundup for Burl Talley at Rafter O, and gambled the money away in one night, so I was told. Maybe you can talk him into going back to where he belongs. To Center Fire with his father and mother. Julia Whipple is heartbroken over losing her son this way."

"I doubt that either Doug or Amos Whipple would appreciate my interfering," Steve said. "Both of them have minds of their own in matters concerning themselves."

The oil lamps were lighted in the coaches. Dusk deepened, and the train climbed from sagebrush into higher country of scrub cedar. And still higher into timber. The clean aroma of pines and firs came on the breeze which turned cool and penetrating.

Presently the train pulled into the siding at Three Forks to lay over for the passage of the southbound train out of Bugle. The stopping point was a dark, deserted flag station which had only the body of a converted box car as a depot. From this point Steve's and Eileen's ranches on Canteen Creek were less than ten miles away to the northwest of the railroad route, while Bugle itself was still a dozen miles farther up the basin.

Burl Talley appeared. "How about a little exercise, Eileen?" he said. "We'll probably be hung up here awhile. Might as well get out and stroll a little."

She arose. "Of course."

Talley said evenly, "Will you join us, Santee?"

"Thanks," Steve said. "Maybe later." He was surprised that Talley had treated him with that courtesy.

The majority of the passengers alighted also. Steve followed them. He rolled a smoke and stood in darkness near the coaches. Eileen and Talley walked past on the clay platform. She was resting a hand on Talley's arm. Steve heard her laugh, enjoying some remark he had made.

Louie Latzo and his companions also moved past. They had retrieved their six-shooters. Latzo gave Steve a gray and promising look.

The stop ended and the strollers filed aboard. The passengers were impatient now to reach Bugle after their long day's ride. The bottles were empty and they were hungry. They settled down for another siege of boredom.

Eileen again seated herself beside Steve, taking the place nearest the window. Burl Talley frowned, not at all pleased, and was forced to join Amos Whipple in the seat ahead.

26

Eileen leaned her head against the worn back of the plush seat and said, "I'm drowsy."

The train lurched into motion, crawling out of the siding, and the engine labored for traction on a slight upgrade.

Full darkness had fallen. Steve watched flickering glow from the firebox play against the timber and boulders along the right of way as the fireman fed fuel beneath the boiler.

The throb of the smokestack began to quicken and steady as the train gained momentum. Abruptly this broke off completely. The cars slowed and came to a jarring stop.

The majority of the passengers were dozing. Some muttered querulous complaints at this new delay. A few peered impatiently out, but when their eyes met only the blank wall of darkness they settled back apathetically.

Tim Foley, the rawboned, brick-topped conductor, went hurrying ahead through the car, scowling in perplexity. The stolid inertia of a train halted in the middle of nowhere bore down.

Steve sat staring past the dozing Eileen out into the darkness, not seeing the blackness, not seeing anything, for his thoughts were on what lay ahead of him when he arrived at Bugle.

A shape, dimly reached by the bands of lamplight from the coach windows moved across his line of vision. Preoccupied, his mind remotely noted the fact that it was a person on foot, walking alongside the train.

He was struck by the impression of something unusual in the shape of that figure, and he leaned forward across Eileen to peer from the window. His movement aroused her and she opened her eyes and turned to see what had attracted his interest.

At that moment the door of the firebox was opened again. For a few seconds the landscape was bathed in crimson light. Then the lightning-like flicker was shut off.

Steve sat motionless. Eileen uttered a tiny sound. In that brief play of firelight they had found themselves gazing at not one but two figures alongside the train. They were no more than a dozen yards away, moving parallel with the coaches in the direction of the engine ahead.

The picture remained clear in Steve's mind. He wondered if it had been imagination. His gaze jerked to Eileen and he saw that it was not, for he understood that she had seen the same thing.

Those two figures out there could have been something from a dream. Or a nightmare. One, at least, had been something hard to believe. A yellow slicker, and cheap white canvas gloves. A gray, shapeless mass for a head. And no face.

Steve knew that what he had seen was a masked man—a man who had a canvas bag, with eyeholes, pulled over his head and shoulders. His gloved hands had carried a sawed-off shotgun, and around his waist had been two holstered pistols and a belt of cartridges.

The other intruder had been nearer the coach. He was taller than the first, wider of shoulders and with the carriage of a younger man. He also had been muffled in a slicker and cotton gloves, and had carried a rifle and a brace of pistols.

But, a moment before the firebox had opened, this one had evidently walked into the entanglement of a half-dead scrub cedar and one of the dead snags had caught the canvas hood and had lifted it from his head. The man was in the act of frantically trying to readjust it when the firelight had revealed him.

Both Steve and Eileen had only the briefest glimpse of his features, and that had been only a profile view. He was a good-looking man of about Steve's own age and with thick, fair hair.

The blackness held. Steve saw the wide, horrified disbelief commence in Eileen, and grow. They sat looking at each other. Neither wanted to speak.

The remainder of the passengers still drowsed. Evidently what Steve and Eileen had seen had escaped the notice of the others.

Guns began exploding ahead! Steve now saw the two masked men once more, outlined against the flashes of powder flame which seemed to be originating near the engine. The taller one had drawn the concealing hood over his head. He and his companion began shooting into the air over the tops of the coaches.

"Stay where you are an' you won't git hurt!" a shrill, disguised voice shouted.

Chapter
Four

The engine stack broke into thundering life. Steve could hear the drive wheels spinning, as though an inexperienced hand was at the throttle. Steam roared.

The passengers, aroused from their lethargy, were still blinking confusedly, unable to rationalize events.

Someone lifted his voice. "Lord a'mighty! It's a stick-up, as shore as little apples. I was in the one near Rock Springs last spring. They're holdin' up the express car!"

Amos Whipple lurched to his feet. "The express car? Our beef money! Our money! That's what they're after!"

That started a stampede for the doors. But the first man to reach the outer platform recoiled, for bullets were sweeping along the sides of the coaches, laying a grim deadline.

The disguised voice arose again. "Stay inside, or you'll stop some lead, you fools! This is none of your affair. We won't bother you."

The aisle was blocked by frantic cattlemen. The grating of a released coupling pin came and the coaches lurched slightly, then became motionless again.

"Damn them, they've cut off the express car!" Amos Whipple bellowed. "Stop them! Get out of my way!"

"Easy!" a man on the platform protested. "We'll get killed if we go out there."

Another voice in the car was raised. "Use your heads, men! After all, this is the express company's responsibility. It's their problem. They'll have to pay off. Why risk your lives unnecessarily?"

Steve could not be sure, but he believed that voice belonged to Burl Talley. Evidently it seemed like logic to some of the less reckless men, and the surge for the doors lost enthusiasm.

But Amos Whipple was in no mood to listen. He was blocked in the jammed aisle. He stood frothing and shouting for a clear path. His words were almost unintelligible. His helplessness seemed to drive him into a frenzy.

He turned and backed into the space between seats and turned to the window as though of a mind to attempt to descend by that route from the car. Then he glimpsed the two masked men outside. They had now broken into a run and were on their way forward, evidently to board the engine or the express car, which was pulling away.

Amos Whipple was armed. He snatched out his six-shooter and leveled it. The taller of the two train bandits was an easy target through the open window and his back was to the cattleman.

Steve leaned over the seat and jostled Amos's elbow an instant before the hammer fell. The gun exploded, but the bullet went wild. Before Whipple could recover his balance to fire again, his quarry had vanished out of range.

Amos whirled and glared. When he realized that it was Steve who had interfered, he at first turned white with fury, then crimson. For the space of a heartbeat Steve expected to be shot down by the infuriated man.

Eileen tried to move in front of him, but Steve would not permit that. "It was an accident, Uncle Amos!" she exclaimed. "Steve started to crowd past me and through the window to fight them. He bumped your arm."

Amos knew it could not have happened that way. He started to say something to Eileen, then decided against it.

A final volley of shots crashed along the cars. The throb of the engine stack increased. This settled to a steady sound, which began to recede ahead.

"They're gittin' away!" a man said hoarsely. "They're steamin' away with the express car, just like they did twice before. It must be the same bunch."

Amos Whipple glared at Steve, his eyes blazing. "You—you——!" he said. He raised his six-shooter.

He would have fired, but Eileen frantically pushed the gun down.

Burl Talley came fighting his way through the throng, attracted by the commotion. "What's wrong?" he exclaimed. "Amos! Good Lord! Quit it! What's happened?"

Amos Whipple, with an effort, gained control of his rage. He lowered the gun and finally holstered it. He gazed at Steve for a moment or two longer, his eyes bleak and condemning.

He turned away without answering Talley. Together they shouldered their way down the aisle, following the wild-eyed, confused men of the Pool, who were now spilling from the coaches onto the dark right of way.

There they milled around, stumbling into the ditches and over crossties. Tim Foley, so excited his voice sounded like a child's tin whistle, kept chattering, "What are we goin' to do, me boys? 'Tis a terrible thing that's happened this night to Conductor Tim Foley's train. Now, what are we goin' to do?"

Steve remained sitting in the coach. He knew it was a waste of energy to do anything else. Afoot, it was hopeless to think of attempting pursuit of the outlaws.

Eileen sat with him. Suddenly she uttered a little startled sound. "Your money! It—it was in the express car too!"

"It's gone," he said. "Along with your beef money. But, as someone said, the express company will make it good. That's the least of my worries."

"Yes," she said. "I know what you mean. I—I wish we hadn't been looking in a certain direction at a certain time."

They dropped that subject and sat without speaking. Steve was sure Amos Whipple believed he had been an accomplice in the holdup and a member of the outlaw band.

After some time the slam of a dynamite explosion drifted from far away. The sound rolled across the basin to the Powderhorns and returned after a surprising interval as a faint rumble.

"This'll cost Northern Express a pretty penny," a rancher said. "There was plenty more'n our eighty thousand dollars in that car. I seen 'em load a bank box aboard at Cheyenne, an' they put another treasure box into the car at Junction Bend."

"It might not cost Northern Express anything," Burl Talley said.

A dozen voices spoke at once. "What's that? What do you mean, Burl?"

"I hope I'm wrong," Talley said reluctantly. "But I'm wondering if Northern Express can pay off."

Utter silence came for an instant that was broken by a wild babble of excited questions.

Talley finally could make himself heard again. "I happen to know that Northern Express had trouble making good on the last holdup," he said. "It's a small company, you know, and owned by a few private individuals. It's not backed by any of the big express companies."

"Do you realize what you're sayin', Burl?" Amos Whipple shouted.

"Only too well," Talley said. "And I hope I'm dead wrong."

"Why—why I couldn't stand to lose that beef money," a cattleman said. "Nor could a lot of the other boys. It's set us back to where we was when Buck Santee robbed us. Some of us will go under."

"I'm in the same boat with you," Talley said. "I have some money in the beef pool too. But I thought it best that we face the truth. You men all seem to be so sure this robbery didn't mean a thing to you. Maybe you'll get off your hip pockets now and try to find these robbers."

Steve looked at Eileen. "Looks like the Pool will have to wait awhile after all before I can pay back that ten thousand dollars."

The cattlemen were a frenzied, howling mass, shouting threats and recriminations. One shook a fist in Amos Whipple's face. "You was the one that talked us into sendin' the money in the express car!" he frothed. "You must have knowed Northern Express was shaky. You're one of the big augurs in the basin."

"How would I know it?" Amos said bitterly. "Don't you go blamin' me. I figured the money'd be safer in an express safe than among a pack o' whiskey-soaked sots like you cowmen. They'd have taken it from you whether it was here or there. I didn't see any of you wantin' to stand up ag'in them. I'll smash in the mouth of the first man who says another word ag'in me."

Then he added hoarsely. "We'll get that money back whether the express company makes good or not. I promise you that. An' I'll hang these outlaws higher'n Haman. That's another promise you can bank on."

"Do you figger you're smarter'n the law?" a rancher demanded. "This is the third train that's been robbed an' we all know danged well there must be express detectives workin' in this country since the first job. But nobody's catched anyone, has they? Ain't seen hide nor hair of these slick cusses. An' now here's a new stick-up pulled right under their noses. Are you sharper'n the Pinkertons an' federal marshals?"

"Smart enough not to bray back when a jackass brays at me," Amos snorted. "I know what I know, but I'll only tell it at the right time an' place. An' that won't be in any court-room where slick lawyers throw snakey loops. It'll be in front of the kind of a jury whose only verdicts will be exoneration or the hang-rope."

An uneasy silence came. "That's mighty strong talk, Amos," Burl Talley said.

Amos Whipple had voiced the Vigilante creed, a creed that had been invoked in violent and sanguine cleanups of other frontier towns and other ranges.

"Strong talk's what's needed," Amos snapped. "We all know what's been happenin' in Bugle, but we closed our eyes to it because we wasn't hit directly. Outlaws, scoundrels, fancy women, and all the other scum of the West have come since the mines hit it rich. Shootin's, robberies, an' general all-around cussedness."

"Bill Rawls ought to be able——"

"Bill Rawls is a good, honest sheriff an' has done his best," Amos said. "So has the town marshal, but the job is too big for 'em. That's plain enough now. We all know in our hearts that this gang of train robbers likely has their nest right near Bugle, but because it wasn't our own ox that was gored we didn't give a hoot. Now it's our pocketbooks that stand to be flattened just when we was seein' our way out of the woods for keeps. We got hit by lightnin'. But there's ways of strikin' back. An' ways of gittin' our money back."

"How?" men shouted eagerly.

"I'll tell that too, at the right time an' the right place that I mentioned," Amos said.

Steve was aware that Eileen had moved closer to him as they listened. She was pale, her eyes dark with the weight of her knowledge. She suddenly seemed to reach a decision. She started to arise. Steve caught her arm, halting her.

"You can't do it," he said. "*We* can't do it."

"He's making Vigilante talk," she said. "He means it. You know how that works. A summary court under a hang-tree where they have you convicted before you can say a word. They strike fast and don't listen to reason. They're as likely to hang an innocent man as a guilty one."

"You can't do what you have in mind," he said.

She sank back into the seat. They were silent for a time. She looked at him. She was shaking now. "You know you should never have stopped me," she said. "Don't you?"

33

He didn't answer. They were thinking of the likeable comrade of their childhood who had shared their joys and their sorrows. Doug Whipple.

For the face of the train bandit which they had glimpsed during the holdup was the face of that same person.

Steve, in jostling Amos Whipple's gun arm had saved the Center Fire owner from the horror of killing his own son.

"Whatever are we going to do?" Eileen asked.

"Forget what you saw," he said.

"Will you forget also?"

He smiled wryly. "That might be a little difficult. From what was said there's a lot more than the Pool's eighty thousand dollars and my thirteen thousand involved. And I'm suspected in having had a hand in stealing it. However, you're not to get mixed up in this, young lady. You never saw a thing tonight."

There was a look in her face and a little set to her mouth that brought back memories of other days when he and Doug had tried determinedly to bar her from their more reckless ventures. "Go to Antler and stay there," he said.

Her expression did not change. "Damn it!" he said. "You look just like you used to when Doug and I would try to shake you off when we wanted to go somewhere without having a brat like you tagging along."

"Go to your own ranch and hole up," she said tartly. "And I will do as I please."

"Just as you've always done," he said.

"You can't boss me around, Steve Santee. I'm not a child anymore."

"Nobody could tell you what to do even when you were a child. You always were as onery as a bogged cow."

Burl Talley entered the car and came striding up. "A hell of a mess, Eileen," he said. "Whoever pulled this holdup had it well planned. My guess is that one or two of them slipped aboard the engine during the stop at Three Forks. The others waited here. All of them pulled out with the engine and the express car, and we can't do a thing about it until they begin to worry about us at Bugle and send out to investigate. Tim Foley says the telegraph line has been short-circuited."

She arose and walked with Talley out of the car. She looked back at Steve and nodded. "Just as I've always done," she said.

Chapter
Five

It was nearly midnight before an engine arrived from Bugle, bringing Sheriff Bill Rawls and half a dozen possemen, along with a carload of saddle horses.

The details of the holdup began to fall into place. The engineer and fireman had been slugged by masked men who evidently had boarded the engine at Three Forks, as Burl Talley had surmised. The trainmen had been blindfolded and tied hand and foot.

After detaching the express car from the train the outlaws had drawn it a mile away and then had given the messenger his choice of surrendering or being blown sky high with dynamite. The leader of the outlaws had used the same disguised voice they all had heard.

The messenger had preferred to stay alive. He had obeyed orders to alight from the car, and in the darkness had scarcely even glimpsed his captors. He had been bound and gagged and he and the train crew had been left lying alongside the right of way at the point where they were sighted and picked up by the sheriff aboard the rescue train later on.

The outlaws had steamed away with the express car. Some five miles farther on they had dynamited the safe and looted it. They had then abandoned the engine and car, but had left the throttle open on the locomotive. It had been found, along with the shattered car, only a mile from Bugle, steam down and the boiler fires nearly out.

Steve heard Bill Rawls say that it was believed there had been around one hundred and thirty thousand dollars, all told, in the express safe. It was one of the richest hauls in the history of train robbery.

"The worst of it," Rawls said, "is that nobody is likely to find out just where they left the train with the money. We know where they blew the safe. There was wreckage around. But they probably stayed with the engine and got off somewhere between that point and Bugle. That's ten miles."

"It's the same stunt they pulled on the other two jobs," Burl Talley said.

"They figured out a way to light where they won't leave any trail," Rawls said. "Come daybreak we'll go over that stretch of track 'til our eyes bulge, an' we won't see even a footprint to tell us anything."

Ashen-faced cattlemen who faced a bleak winter now that they had lost their season's profits remained at the scene to join the posses when daylight came. The majority of the passengers rode on into Bugle aboard the coaches.

Steve rode with them. He had stayed in the background during the noisy and sometimes dangerous hours while awaiting the sheriff. At times he had been aware that the suspicion and anger his presence aroused had neared the explosive point.

Amos Whipple also was with the townbound group. He had been the heaviest loser in the robbery, for his Center Fire beef had accounted for nearly a third of the eighty thousand dollars in the Pool's beef money.

He had been silent since making the threat of Vigilante vengeance. He was not an obtuse man, and he was so careful to act as though he had lost interest in Steve that it was evident the opposite was true.

Eileen sat with Burl Talley across the aisle, for Louie Latzo and his pals had shifted to the other coach. She was wan and tired now, drained by the stress of the holdup and the sleepless night, and burdened by the knowledge that she and Steve shared.

Steve was positive that only he and Eileen had been gazing out of the car at the moment Doug Whipple had been surprised by the fire glow with his mask removed.

She finally dozed off. Talley drew her head over upon his shoulder. She aroused, looked up at him speculatively for a moment. She pulled away then. But she smiled at him. However, after that she remained awake.

Steve felt the strain also. The loss of the money seemed unimportant to him. This, he candidly admitted, was because he had looked upon himself only as its custodian and not its owner.

The gold was only incidental. A factor of far greater value was involved. The fact was that he possessed the means of recovering not only his own fund, but the Pool's money also. That means had a name. The name was Doug Whipple.

That brought back the memory of a day when he had dangled, terrified, from a ledge a hundred feet above a rapids on the Powderhorn River with Doug clinging to his wrists.

They had been fourteen years of age at the time and he had been demonstrating his daredeviltry by walking the lip of the sloping ledge above the rapids. He had slipped. Only Doug's swiftness in getting within reaching distance had saved him from falling at once to his death.

He remembered the way Doug's feet had slid a fraction of an inch at a time toward the rim of the ledge, with the loose, decomposing granite giving way little by little. He remembered the look in Doug's eyes. Doug had made up his mind to hang on and go over to death with him if it came to that rather than release his grip.

Then Doug's toes had found firm support on a solid crevice. That had been enough. With a last surge of their combined strength Steve had clawed his way back to safety.

Even after the years Steve found himself sweating a little and breathing hard as he lived over that moment. He owed his life to the man he had seen a few hours earlier wearing an outlaw's mask. Even above that he and Doug Whipple had been comrades. Friends. As boys they had taken a blood oath as brothers.

He watched the lights of Bugle rise out of the timber in the distance as the train rumbled over the switch frogs into the station.

The town was bigger. It was three in the morning and in the old days Bugle would have been abed and dark long since. Now lights still glittered in gambling houses and dancehalls that had sprung up for several blocks from the depot on Bozeman Street. Front Street, still a single-sided thoroughfare facing the railroad tracks, which had been given over in the past to shacks and mule yards, was now occupied by dimly-lit honky-tonks, gambling houses and brothels.

Steve alighted. When he walked into Bozeman Street he found scarcely a familiar landmark. The business district had been pushed back half a dozen blocks from the depot and this section was crowded with higher-class gambling houses and saloons than the type on Front Street. The sedate part of town was dark now and peaceful. Here and there

37

the brighter glow of late eating places and hotels offered signs of life.

The gay district nearer at hand was still doing business. There was noisy drunken revelry in a dancehall. Somewhere on Front Street arose the pounding of feet and shouting and screaming as a fight broke out.

Steve had not anticipated changes as drastic as this. He stood, his war sack over his shoulder, gazing perplexed, seeking some link with the past. Then he sighted the swinging, lighted sign marking Jeb Keene's white-painted hostelry, the Pioneer House. It was several blocks away.

Burl Talley had appropriated the only hansom cab available at the depot and was helping Eileen aboard with her luggage. Amos Whipple joined them, and the driver stirred the horse into action. The equipage went clattering away, heading for the Pioneer House.

The remainder of the train arrivals were scattering, the majority of them streaming toward the nearest saloon to drink and talk over the robbery.

Steve's throat was powder dry. He stopped at the last open bar, which was nearly deserted, and drank beer with the deep gratitude of a thirsty man.

He walked onward past the office of Burl Talley's lumberyard toward the Pioneer House up the street. The hotel occupied the corner of an intersection. Light spilled onto the sidewalk from the lamp over the clerk's desk in the lobby.

As he neared the place Burl Talley emerged alone, boarded the hansom, and the driver swung the vehicle around in the street and headed for the lumber office. There Talley had always maintained living quarters.

Steve crossed the street and stepped on the sidewalk in front of the Pioneer House.

A voice said, "Get him!" Three men came at him, rising from the shadows at the corner of the building where they had been crouching in wait.

He saw the sideburned Louie Latzo leaping at him, teeth ashine in a grin of anticipation. He knew then that the other two must be the hard-cased pair of the train journey, Al Painter and Chick Varney.

He lurched aside, sending the war sack whirling at Latzo's legs. That upset the man, tripping him so that he came plunging forward into the half-raised uppercut that Steve had started. He felt his knuckles loosen teeth.

Then Al Painter's bulk was on his back, knees hammering into him. Varney came in, smashing at his face with both fists while Painter tried to pin down his arms.

He reeled backwards and rammed Painter against the wall of the building. He dove forward in a somersault, grasping the man's arms and carrying him whirling with him. Painter crashed into the street with a grunting, breath-taking jar.

Steve came to his feet and was met by a smash to the face by Varney. At the same time Louie Latzo loomed over him, swinging the muzzle of a six-shooter. Steve partly evaded the gun, but the blow glanced off the point of his shoulder and he felt the shock drive down the nerves of his left arm, leaving it momentarily numb.

Varney was flailing at him and Al Painter, shaken, but more savage than ever was coming back into the fight against him.

He couldn't hold them off much longer. He wanted to damage Latzo above all, before he went under. He weaved, braced himself, found his opening and drove a sledging smash into the man's face. Latzo reeled back, blood spurting.

Steve paid for that. Both Painter and Varney were hammering blows to his face and body. He fought, but his strength was draining rapidly, for he had expended it with blast furnace fury during these hectic moments. He began to go down and he knew they would beat and kick him to pulp once they had him beneath their boots.

Help arrived. Al Painter was snatched away from him. He heard the thud of a fist and Painter went staggering. The arrival followed his target into the doorlight from the hotel.

It was Doug Whipple. He was hatless and wore a natty double-breasted shirt with pearl buttons. He had on foxed saddle breeches and new cowboots. His fair hair was waving like a banner and there was delight in his face as he moved in on Al Painter, his fists darting.

"Damn you, Al!" he said. "Three of you on Steve!"

Painter was far from done for. "Why are you dealin' yourself in on this, Whipple?" he panted.

Chick Varney left Steve, believing he was no longer a problem and lunged toward Doug. A girl darted down the steps from the door of the hotel. "Oh, no, you don't!" Eileen's voice sounded.

She was swinging the heavy ledger which she had seized from the clerk's desk. That ledger carried names of guests dating back for forty years. It came crashing down on Chick Varney's head with the sound of a mallet on a stake.

Varney stood an instant, his knees unsteady. He sat down carefully, as though not sure of his plans. Then he keeled over.

Steve arose in time to intercept Louie Latzo, who had decided to come back into the fight and was about to leap on Doug Whipple's back. He drove a punch to Louie's body. The man whirled, went staggering aside, and fell into the street on his face.

Al Painter was backing away from Doug. No guns had been drawn during the fight, but that thought was in Painter's mind now. Steve, realizing his intention, kept driving ahead, carried by the momentum of the finishing blow he had dealt Latzo. He crashed into Painter, pitching him backwards to the sidewalk. As they fell he smashed an elbow into the man's throat.

That took the last of the fight out of Al Painter. He lay gagging and wheezing.

Steve dragged himself to his feet. He wasn't in much better shape than Painter. He looked at Doug Whipple. "She always did insist on horning in on our fun," he said. "It's just like old times."

He and Doug stood grinning foolishly at each other. Steve became aware of blood dripping from his chin. A sleeve of his coat was torn and he was matted with gore and dust. Perspiration now began to pour from him. But Doug seemed unmarked and unruffled.

Eileen dropped the bulky ledger and sat down shakily on the steps. Evidently she had been preparing for bed when the sound of the brawl had brought her from her room, for she had loosened her hair, and it hung down in a coppery cascade over her shoulders.

"I—I didn't k—kill that man, did I?" she chattered.

"Deader than a tombstone," Steve said. "You'll likely get hung for it."

"I always said she'd come to a bad end," Doug said.

"I didn't mean to hit him that hard," Eileen wailed.

Chick Varney was far from dead. He stirred and lifted himself dazedly to a sitting position.

"The stampede went right over you," Doug told him.

Louie Latzo pulled himself to hands and knees and crawled to safer distance. He got to his feet and began uttering profanity and threats.

Painter also lurched to his feet. "Shut up!" he snarled at Latzo. "If you'd fight as well with your fists as your mouth . . ."

Painter then looked at Doug and said, "You do the damnedest things, Whipple."

"I think so myself," Doug said.

Painter and Varney walked shakily away, nursing their injuries. Louie Latzo followed them, a hand to his broken, bleeding nose.

Amos Whipple came charging from the hotel. He was in his undershirt, his suspenders flapping. Other guests were arriving also. Heads had appeared at doors and windows.

Amos pulled up. He gave Steve a glare, then wheeled on his son. "You?" he said. "I might have known you'd be mixed up in any cheap street brawl that took place."

He glowered at Eileen. "And what are you doing here, young lady?"

"The trouble started right beneath my window," she said. "So I came down to see what was going on."

"An' she joined in the ruckus," said Jeb Keene, the hotel owner. "She knocked out one of 'em with my register." Jeb added proudly, "That ain't the fust time thet book's been used to whack somebody over the haid. Fact is, I've slammed down a few with it myself. But I don't ever recollect that a lady ever swung it in a brawl before."

He gazed admiringly at Eileen. "I'll make a note of it in the page for special events," he said.

"Thank you," Eileen said. "I have always wanted to do something that would go down in history."

Amos Whipple was in no mood for light talk. "Go to your room," he said grimly. "You've made enough of a spectacle of yourself for one night. If your dad and your mother were alive how would they feel about you getting mixed up in a thing like this?"

Burl Talley arrived. "Why, Eileen!" he exclaimed. "What's happened?"

"It seems like we were in a fight," Eileen said.

She moved close to Steve and peered at his face. "You look very much like it," she said. "Come inside where I can take a better view of the damage. You seem to have been hit by several things much more bruising than a book. That eye is a dandy, and you're bleeding nicely from that gash on your jaw, not to mention other items."

She added seriously, "You may have some broken bones."

Amos Whipple started to protest, but she grasped Steve's arm and tried to steer him toward the door of the hotel. Steve resisted. "I'll go to a saloon and——" he began.

"And be beat up again by some of Latzo's hoodlums," she said.

She led him into the hotel and on through the dark dining room into the kitchen. "Light a lamp and fetch water and towels, court plaster and liniment and alum and whatever else you have in stock," she ordered.

Jeb Keene hurried to obey. Steve suffered her to use warm water on his injuries. She applied liniment and alum and winced with him when he grimaced at the sting. She used a strip of court plaster on his jaw.

Doug sat by, smoking a cigarette and watching. Burl Talley was the only other bystander. He remained in the background, waiting patiently for Eileen, who was being helped in her task by Jeb Keene. Amos Whipple had not followed them.

She finished with Steve. "You'll have a scar on that jawbone of yours, I'm afraid," she said. "But you escaped better than I had expected. Your beauty won't be too badly blemished."

She walked to Doug and inspected him carefully. "They barely mussed your hair," she said. "You always were one to come out of trouble looking like you'd been to a pink tea. Please tell me the secret. I always get hot and wild-looking, and the freckles pop out something awful."

"I waited until Steve had 'em licked, an' then came in with bugles blowing," Doug said.

She lifted his hands and peered. "At least you bear the marks of honorable combat," she said. "You've got some barked knuckles and one is puffing. You should have rammed this into cold water before this. Why didn't you say something about it?"

"Quit poking it!" Doug protested. "Ouch! Lord a'mighty,

42

Eileen! Take it easy. Lucky for me it's not my roping hand."

"Or your poker or drinking hand," Eileen said. "Here! Put it in this water. Hold it there until I say to take it out."

Doug looked at Steve. "If I resisted she'd probably whack me with the ledger an' stretch me out like a calf at brandin'," he said.

Chapter Six

Any impression that three years had left Doug untouched faded under the glare of the lamplight. His features had thickened a trifle and there was an opaque, lifeless quality in his eyes, as though he had walled in his thoughts.

He was still handsome. His lips were perhaps thinner and tighter and there was the slight blurring of his features —the mark of hard living, hard drinking, and of harsh and tense emotions beneath the surface.

Steve searched his mind for something casual to say, something that would not betray the fact that he knew that Doug, who had saved his life in the past and had within the last few minutes joined in to save him from being beaten, perhaps to death, had also, on this same night, helped hold up a train and rob him and other men of the Powderhorn. Above all, he had robbed his own father.

It did not seem possible that the slicker-clad outlaw whose face he had glimpsed could be the same Doug Whipple who stood so obedient to Eileen's orders, grinning down at her fondly. It was evident that all the recollections of the joyful days of their childhood were in his mind, as they had been in Steve's.

But he was one and the same man. It could not have been an error of resemblance. Eileen had seen him also, and Steve knew she was keeping her eyes away from him now as she worked on his damaged hands, because in her, no doubt, was the same incredulity that was in him. She did not want Doug to suspect her dark bewilderment.

Doug's presence in Bugle meant that he had come directly to town after the robbery. That indicated that his companions also were here in Bugle, mingling with the townfolk as honest citizens.

Steve became aware that Doug was watching him. Doug's expression had shifted a trifle as though a disturbing thought had crossed his mind. He swung his glance away. He said to Eileen, "The hand feels much better. It's surprising what a little liniment and a lot of sympathy does for a man."

Mart Lowery, town marshal of Bugle, came hurrying into the kitchen, followed by several men who seemed to be there out of mere curiosity. One of these bystanders was blocky-shouldered and square-faced, with a clipped graying mustache. He wore a commonplace dark serge suit, and high-heeled cowboots and a stiff-brimmed, dented range hat.

Mart Lowery had worn the shield of the law for years. He was past sixty now, frosted at the temples, and more of a mind to live out his full span of life rather than delve deep for trouble. There was a wariness and also distaste in the inspection he gave Steve. Lean and big-boned, he had a large nose and a drooping mustache.

He spoke respectfully to Talley. "Howdy, Burl."

He touched his hat to Eileen. "Surprised to see you here, Miss Maddox," he said.

His greeting to Doug Whipple was strictly neutral. "How did you get mixed up in this, Doug?" he asked.

"It looked a little one-sided," Doug said.

"That depends," Lowery said.

Steve knew then that the marshal had been coached and primed by Amos Whipple. He surmised that Amos had hinted that he believed Steve was implicated in the train holdup or at least had guilty knowledge as to the perpetrators.

"What started it, Santee?" Mart Lowery asked without preliminary. He had been friendly with Steve's father in the days when Buck Santee was chairman of the Powderhorn Pool and therefore a man to be reckoned with. But he was hostile now.

"An antelope with a broken leg," Steve said.

Lowery frowned. "Let's pass up the small talk an' get down to cases. I understand you an' Louie had trouble on the train. He's got a broken nose an' maybe a busted jaw. Not that I grieve none for him. Nor for Al Painter or Chick Varney. They're mussed up considerable also. They're down

44

at Doc Skelley's office gettin' patched up. I asked you what started it?"

"I've already told you," Steve said.

Eileen spoke. "Latzo took some shots at——"

"I'll do my own talking," Steve said to her. And to the marshal, "What difference does it make what started it? It started. That's all."

"Not much difference, I reckon," Lowery said. "But I'm a lot more interested in how it's likely to end. Louie has a brother who don't like to see his kinfolk pushed around. Nick Latzo plays rough. I'm warnin' you, Santee, not to bring your feuds into Bugle—particularly here in the respectable part of town. I don't want any gunplay either here or down along the tracks. A train stick-up an' a street fight the first night you hit town ought to be about enough."

"Meaning that you think I had something to do with the train robbery?" Steve asked.

"I didn't say that," Lowery protested hastily. "All I'm sayin' is that I'm here to keep the peace in Bugle. An' I don't want any grudges poppin' up."

Eileen had been listening with growing indignation. "Has it ever occurred to anyone, Mart Lowery, that we members of the Pool weren't the only losers in that holdup?" she burst out. "Steve Santee had quite a sum of his own money in that express safe also."

"Yeah?" Lowery said skeptically. "How much?"

Steve tried to halt her, but there was no silencing her. "Thirteen thousand dollars!"

Lowery started to laugh disbelievingly. That died off. Something in Steve's eyes warned him that scoffing might be dangerous.

Amos Whipple came stomping into the kitchen through a side door beyond which he had been lurking, listening to what had been said. Eileen's revelation had startled him into appearing.

"What's that?" he demanded. "What kind of nonsense is this, Santee, about you losing thirteen thousand dollars? Ridiculous!"

Doug spoke. "Some day, Dad, you're going to get your nose caught in a door, eavesdropping on people."

Amos glared at his son, then ignored him. "You don't expect us to believe a story like that, do you?" he said to Steve.

45

"I'm not interested in whether you believe it or not, Amos," Steve said.

"Eileen, did you see any of this money Santee claims he had?" Amos demanded. "With your own eyes, I mean?"

"No," she said. "Not with my own eyes. But it was there. What object would Steve have in lying?"

Amos started to blurt out an answer to that, then thought better of it. "That remains to be seen," he said.

Burl Talley moved up and laid a hand on Eileen's arm. "You must be very tired, my dear," he said. "You had better get some sleep. Tomorrow may be a long day. They'll be turning this range upside down, hunting those devils who robbed us. I'm going to join in myself, this time. I've got some of my own money at stake now. Odd how it changes a man's viewpoint when his own toes are stepped on. Up to now, like everyone else, I've let the law officers do all the work, figuring that's what they were paid for."

He looked at Amos. "Maybe you were right, Amos, in what you said about it being high time that citizens take a hand in cleaning up the Powderhorn."

"Yes," Amos said tersely. "Yes."

Mart Lowery glanced uneasily from face to face. Once more the threat of Vigilante action had been made. And the backing of a man of Talley's prominence added great power to the blackening storm.

"Thirteen thousand dollars is quite a jag of money to lose, if the express company can't pay off," Amos said to Steve. "You seem to be takin' it right calmly."

"If I look calm then appearances are very misleading, and that's for sure," Steve said. "I earned that money with more sweat and strain than I ever thought I'd go through for any man or anything."

"If you really had any such amount, I reckon I can guess where you got the most of it about three years ago," Amos said.

Eileen uttered an outraged gasp. "That isn't fair, Uncle Amos! And it isn't true! Why, Steve intended to turn ten thousand dollars of that money over to——"

Steve halted her. "It's no use," he said.

But she rushed on. "Steve was going to give it to the Powderhorn Pool to make up for what was lost the night his father disappeared."

"What?" Amos said derisively. "You don't actually believe that do you, my dear girl?"

"Yes, I do," she said.

Amos took her arm. "It's high time you got some sleep. You better go to your room."

She sighed resignedly, realizing that debate was a waste of time. Talley followed as she let Amos lead her toward the door. He turned and spoke to Steve. "Maybe you'd like to ride posse with us tomorrow, Santee," he said.

"I doubt if I'd be welcome," Steve said.

Talley shrugged. "Perhaps you're right. Marshal, if it's in your mind to arrest Doug Whipple on charges of disturbing the peace I'll go bail and also pay fines and costs. Doug's a friend of mine." And in a burst of generosity, he added, "That goes for Santee also, as far as the fines go. After all, he and Doug may have done the town a favor by taking Louie and his pals to a cleaning."

"We'll pay for our own fun, Burl," Doug spoke sharply.

However Mart Lowery hastily disclaimed any intention of arresting anyone. He had come here at Amos Whipple's request to place the heavy frown of the law on Steve. Instead, he had found himself confronted by forces and undercurrents, the sources of which he could not imagine.

"That big lunker is still waiting at Black Rock," Eileen said, pausing at the door. "And I can still beat both of you at laying a fly over that hole where he lives."

"You have just let yourself in for a fishing trip that will humble your pride," Steve said.

She left then, with Amos and Talley. Mart Lowery also followed them out of the kitchen, and the uninvited bystanders departed too, leaving Steve and Doug alone.

"Thanks, fella," Steve said. "Thanks for helping me out. It was beginning to be a very tight fit when you showed up."

"The pleasure was all mine," Doug said.

"Was it?" Steve asked, carefully keeping his tone casual. "I had an impression, from what Al Painter said, that he and the other two might have been friends of yours."

"Acquaintances might be a better way of putting it," Doug said. "I've played poker with 'em. Any one's money is good in a poker game."

"Did you play at Nick Latzo's roadhouse?"

"Where else?" Doug said. "Any particular reason for asking that question?"

"You really ought to pick better poker partners," Steve said.

"And better places in which to play, maybe?" Doug asked.

"I'll buy a drink," Steve said.

They walked out of the Pioneer House and to the bar Steve had first visited. It was ready for closing. Steve's taste was still for beer, but Doug ordered whiskey. He tossed off a drink, poured another and stood, his hat pushed back on his head, revolving the glass thoughtfully in his hand as he absently studied the contents.

"Was that straight about you having thirteen thousand dollars in that express car, Steve?" he asked abruptly.

"Yes," Steve said. "I've got a company receipt to prove it."

"Why didn't you show that receipt to Amos? He didn't believe you had any such amount of money."

"I didn't figure I owed him any explanation," Steve said. "I'll show the receipt to Bill Rawls, if he wants to see it. As sheriff, he's entitled to look at it, if he's interested in my troubles. That I doubt."

"Did you really intend to turn ten thousand over to the Pool?" Doug asked.

Steve sipped his beer. "Yes."

"You always were one hell of a person for paying off any debt you figured you owed. So was your father, from what I know of him, an' what men have told me."

"There's another debt that I haven't forgotten," Steve said. "Remember that day on the ledge above Racehorse Rapids?"

"There's no debt there, and you know it," Doug said impatiently. "You'd have done the same. You know that too."

"Maybe in the matter of the ten thousand dollars it's just pigheaded pride," Steve said. "I look at it from the viewpoint I'm sure Dad would have taken. He would have figured himself responsible and would have tried to pay it back. So I'm doing it for him so that he can sleep easy."

"You figure then that he's dead?" Doug asked.

Steve nodded. "Beyond all doubt. And I'm sure his bones are somewhere in this range, though I guess the chances are they'll never be found. I'm sure he was killed at the same time Henry Thane was murdered."

"Is that why you came back?"

"Yes. It's at least one of the reasons. I like this country.

I belong here and I don't want to be driven out of it. In fact I won't be driven out."

"May heaven help the guilty man if you ever catch up with him," Doug said. "You can be mighty rough, Steve. As you proved tonight. From the signs, whatever you went through while you were away didn't soften you any."

"Nor has time softened your father," Steve said. "Did you know what was meant when Burl Talley mentioned that it was time for citizens to pitch in against lawlessness in the Powderhorn?"

Doug looked at him without speaking.

"Amos is stirring up the ranchers to ride Vigilante," Steve said. "He means it. It must have been talked over by him and others before tonight. Otherwise he wouldn't have come out in the open with it."

Doug tossed off his drink. "Vigilantes!" he said. He laughed. It was dry, bleak humor. "That would be something, wouldn't it? My own father leading the stranglers."

The barkeeper was making a great ceremony of placing chairs on tables and snuffing lamps as a hint that closing time was past.

Steve and Doug walked to the street. The sedate citizens had gone back to bed and the fandango district was quieting at this late hour, although Steve saw that some of the bigger gambling houses evidently never closed their doors or dimmed their lights.

Only a night lamp now burned in the lobby of the Pioneer House a short distance away. All of the guest rooms were dark, but Steve saw a shadow at the window of one of the second-floor quarters. It was a person in a nightgown, and then he realized that it was Eileen. She was there, watching them.

He surmised she had been standing there all the time he and Doug were in the barroom, worrying about them. He knew that Doug had seen also. "She ought to be in bed," he said irritably.

"She always was like a mother hen with us two, tryin' to keep us out of trouble," Doug said. "She's afraid this isn't over yet. She knows Nick Latzo's reputation. You plowed up that leppie brother of his quite deep. Nick will go a far piece out of his way to demonstrate that it doesn't pay to push a Latzo around. Nick is harder formation than Louie. He's been spreading out. He runs the Blue Moon here in town in addition to the roadhouse. That's the one with the revolving blue light on the roof down the street. He lives at the roadhouse but he's at the Blue Moon every night, dealing big poker games. I saw him there not long before you hit town and got yourself into a bushel of trouble."

"It's quite a crowded bushel," Steve said. "You're jammed into it with me."

Doug shrugged. "I didn't touch Louie. I only tussled with Al Painter. Painter and Varney don't count. Nick's got half a dozen like them hangin' around his place. They'd shoot a man in the back for a few dollars."

Steve gazed at the dark window where Eileen had been standing. It stared back vacantly. She had withdrawn. "Burl Talley seems to be doing well," he remarked.

Doug knew the reason for that change of subject. "Yeah," he said. "Burl's got the talent for making money. He's the kind that usually gets anything he goes after."

"You mean Eileen," Steve said, and there was distaste in him. "He wants to marry her. That's easy to see. But what does she think about it?"

"Who knows?" Doug said. "You better ask her."

"I have," Steve said. "I was told to mind my own business."

Doug laughed. "I can believe that. She hasn't been in the habit of talking things over with me lately either, particularly matters concerning Talley's courtship."

There was a forced lightness in him, an obvious attempt to be indifferent and neutral. Steve eyed him, trying to read his thoughts.

"I punched cattle for Burl durin' roundup," Doug said in that same casual manner. "Right now I'm loafin'."

He changed the subject. "Have you got a place to hang out tonight, Steve?"

"I'll take a room at the Pioneer," Steve said. "Tomorrow I'll hire a horse and ride out to the ranch. Eileen says the house still seems to be in fair shape."

"It is," Doug said. "I've lived there a lot, in fact. I went over to the river a couple of days ago an' sat awhile on Black Rock, recalling a lot of things. I caught me a grasshopper an' threw him in that eddy back of the big boulder out in the middle. Something that looked like the front end of a catawampus came up through the clear green water and—zowie! No more grasshopper."

"We'll try it together," Steve said. "The three of us. The day after tomorrow, if possible. I can't hold myself down much longer. I've been thinking of Black Rock ever since I went away. And of a fly rod in my hands. And man, I'd like to taste an elk steak again, thin and cooked fast and juicy. Rolled in flour and——"

"I'll be there and blast you for makin' my mouth water here at two o'clock in the mornin'," Doug said. "I haven't bagged me an elk this year."

He stood a moment thinking. "Every rancher and cowboy in the basin will be out tomorrow, tryin' to cut sign of the bunch that stuck up the train," he said. "And half the men from town. What about you, Steve?"

"You heard me tell Talley I wouldn't be welcome," Steve said. "Any particular reason why I should ride posse?"

"There'll be a reward," Doug said. "There's talk of offering five thousand or more."

"Good night," Steve said. "Don't forget. Black Rock the day after tomorrow. I'll talk to Eileen about it in the morning."

He crossed the street and entered the Pioneer House. When he looked back Doug was not in sight.

The night clerk got up from a cot back of the desk and yawningly led him down the hall to a room on the lower floor toward the rear of the building.

Steve listened to the man's receding footsteps and heard him roll back into the cot with a sigh. He lifted his luggage sack onto the bed, opened it, and brought out his six-shooter and holster and shells.

He got out a cloth and cleaned the gun and tried the action, then loaded all six chambers. He buckled on the belt and slid the gun into the holster.

He left the hotel by way of a rear door, which opened into a side street, for he did not want to disturb the clerk who might not yet be asleep.

He returned to Bozeman Street and walked onward into the gambling district. In some of the places percentage girls were still dancing with miners and cowboys.

He suddenly had the impression of being followed. He turned. A man was strolling the sidewalk, some distance

51

back of him. This person passed the band of light from a doorway and Steve identified him as the blocky, square-jawed man he had noticed earlier during his talk with Mart Lowery. There was nothing furtive about his manner, however, and Steve scoffed at himself for seeing trouble where none existed.

He walked on and entered the door of the gambling house with the revolving light on the roof. Nick Latzo's Blue Moon.

Batteries of ornate oil lamps lighted the place. Cutglass glittered on the backbar and oil paintings of beauties adorned the walls. The card tables had green baize tops. An orchestra of five pieces was playing and there was dancing on a small space at the rear.

Three poker tables were still busy, and from the stacks of chips in sight at least two of the games were for heavy stakes. The players were intent on these games.

The bull-necked Nick Latzo sat at one of the tables and was dealing a stud hand to four opponents. He had grown fleshier and his small eyes were almost hidden in the heavy pouches around them.

Steve's arrival had now been discovered by some of the men who were standing at the bar, among whom were Pool cattlemen who had been aboard the train.

The news spread by means of word and rib-nudging. The orchestra finished its number and prepared to strike up a new tune, but the leader paused, peering and ready to duck to cover. Past experience had taught him that these sudden lulls were often the prelude to stormy moments.

Nick Latzo became aware of the quiet and looked up. He saw Steve and sat watching and waiting, the deck of cards in his hands—his face without tangible expression.

Steve walked down the room to the poker table. The other four players edged back and a plump man pulled in his stomach and began breathing fast, obviously wishing he was somewhere else.

"Hello, Nick!" Steve said.

Latzo did not move. Only his small eyes were active. He was coatless, but wore a vest of green flowered silk over a white silk shirt. A green silk sash was around his thick waist and from this jutted the handle of a scabbarded dagger. He had no gun in sight.

"Well, well, if it isn't Steve Santee himself," Latzo finally spoke. "It's been a long time since you've been in a place of mine. Must be two, three years."

Steve glanced around. The warning had been flashed, for three of Latzo's trouble shooters had appeared and had moved to strategic points in the room. Al Painter, bearing the marks of combat, also emerged from a side door into the main room.

"You know about the little dispute I had with your brother and a couple of your men tonight, of course, Nick?" Steve said.

"They wasn't my men," Latzo said. "They was friends of Louie's. I was told you picked trouble with them."

"If you're taking it up, let's get it over with—right now, Nick," Steve said.

It was so blunt and unexpected that Nick Latzo had no answer ready. Then he saw Steve's purpose. He had not only been taken by surprise, but he had been placed on notice in the presence of many witnesses of being responsible for any foul play that might befall Steve. That was exactly the situation Steve had wanted to create when he had come to the Blue Moon.

Latzo knew he had been outmaneuvered. He had an agile mind back of the blank face, and was quick to attempt to turn the situation in his favor.

"Louie's man enough to settle his own accounts, Santee," he said. "And so am I. Are you huntin' trouble? You must be drunk. Have another one on the house, then go somewhere and sleep it off. You're interferin' with our game."

Steve stood gazing at Latzo a moment. He still felt that among the many dark secrets that Nick Latzo must share with the devious persons who passed through his establishments was the key to what had happened to his father.

Latzo looked back at him, and again his face was utterly without expression. But suddenly Steve was sure he was right. The man knew! He knew Buck Santee's fate.

He realized also that Latzo was fully aware that he, above everything else, would like to pry out that knowledge. He fancied that a faint irony showed briefly in Latzo's eyes, as though daring him to try.

"I'll always make it a point never to be drunk when I'm dealing with you, Nick," Steve said. "And that goes for the present moment as well as the future."

He turned, walked past Latzo's gunmen, and spun a silver

53

dollar on the bar. "I pay for my own drinks when I'm in Nick's place," he told the bartender. "I always have."

He filled a glass from the bottle that was nervously placed before him. He tasted it, then poured it on the floor. "Rotgut," he said. "I'll see you another day, Nick."

He walked through the swing doors to the sidewalk. He pulled up, gazing at Doug Whipple, who stood there. Doug wore a brace of six-shooters and the holsters were tied to his legs with rawhide thongs.

"You do stay up late, fellow," Steve said.

"I knew I had made a mistake when I let it slip that Nick was here in town," Doug shrugged. "You always were one to force the play. I knew you'd go down to the Moon and brace him. Lone-handed. You don't care how young you die, do you? If Nick had lifted a finger they'd have blasted you down. And Louie was aching for 'em to do it. But you got away with it."

"At least, if I'm found with a bullet or a knife in my back or beaten to death out in the brush, Nick will have some embarrassing explaining to do," Steve said. "He'll hear that there's Vigilante talk in the air, if he doesn't already know about it. That'll give him pause for thought. I hope he'll stay clear of me. I need some leeway and don't want to have to spend my time trying to avoid being bushwhacked. You might call this visit to the Blue Moon as setting up a little life insurance. It ought to keep Nick off my back. I've got things to do."

"Such as trying to decide whether to try to help run down the men who held up the train tonight?" Doug asked.

"I've already decided that," Steve said.

Doug stood for a time without speaking. Then he said, "Well, I'll turn in. See you tomorrow, Steve."

"I've taken a room at the Pioneer," Steve said. "There's a spare bed, if you're not fixed up."

"I've got other plans," Doug said.

Steve watched him walk down Bozeman Street and turn into Front Street along the railway tracks. He debated whether to follow Doug and bring him back. Momentarily he had been given an insight into the conflict and turmoil that raged in a man torn between two worlds.

Doug was a person in torment, caught in the demands of loyalty to a friend on the one hand and, on the other, some black necessity which he did not know how to evade. He had gone, Steve knew, to some sordid barroom to drink and dull the poignant sense of guilt that had been so searing in his eyes.

Steve finally turned away. Total weariness was on him as he walked to the Pioneer House. Ahead of him he saw the blocky man enter the hotel. As he walked down the hall to his own room he saw lamplight shining beneath a door near his own. He had the sensation that ears were tuned to his arrival, and to his movements as he prepared to turn in. After he stretched out on the bed he also lay listening for a time. He heard nothing, and finally convinced himself that again it was imagination.

Chapter
Seven

Steve awakened at daybreak and listened to the departure of mounted men who were being assigned by Sheriff Bill Rawls to various sectors of the hills. There was activity in the railroad yards also, and a clatter as a train rolled away. He guessed that it carried more manhunters toward outer points in the basin.

He slept again. The sun was high in the sky when he finally aroused. He arose from bed and the first thing he saw was a white envelope which had been thrust under his door.

It was a plain, cheap envelope and bore no name or writing. It was sealed and he ripped it open, his mind still a trifle fogged with sleep.

He instantly came wide awake. He stood staring at two objects that he had drawn from the envelope. One was a square of paper containing a brief written message which said:

> Santee:
> There are more like the enclosed sample and they'll be easy to earn. Just keep this one on you all the time for quick identification when I get in touch with you.

There was no signature. The note was done in a shaky scrawl which indicated that the wrong writing hand had been used for the sake of disguise.

The other object, which was the "sample" referred to in the note, was a hundred-dollar banknote. It was a well-used bill, and there was no doubt in Steve's mind but that it was genuine.

He read the message again, studying over it. He inspected the torn envelope and tossed it on the dresser, for it told him nothing.

He found himself holding the banknote to the light as though it might reveal some secret message. He grinned wryly at his own confusion.

A hand softly tapped the door at that moment, startling him. He pocketed the banknote, then unlocked the door. His visitor was the blocky, gray-mustached man whom he had suspected of trailing him the previous night. He stared.

"I'd like a word with you," the man said, glancing apprehensively up and down the hall. Then he pushed his way past Steve into the room. "I don't want anybody to know I'm here," he explained.

Steve closed and bolted the door. The man appeared to be about fifty and had eyes that were a pale blue and very direct. He looked around Steve's room. His glance took in the torn envelope on the dresser and Steve fancied that it halted there for an instant. His gaze roved onward and Steve felt that all details were being tabulated in his mind.

His attention returned to Steve. He offered a taut, little smile. "I go by the name of John Drumm in this range," he said. "I'm supposed to be a horse buyer for big livery companies in the east. That gives me an excuse for traveling around and getting acquainted at the ranches."

"Why would you need an excuse for that?" Steve asked carefully.

"My real name is Clum. Frank Clum. I'm a deputy United States Marshal. For the past two months, however, I've been detached for special duty. Right now my salary is being paid by several express companies. All of the express outfits are interested in breaking up any organized gangs of outlaws who rob trains."

"Why are you telling me this?" Steve asked.

"Because I believe we might have the same purpose in mind and might be able to help each other."

"Do you mean catching train robbers?"

"Perhaps. And also in trying to solve the disappearance of your father.

Steve gazed demandingly at him. Clum nodded. "I know all about your search for your father. There's a full report on it in the district headquarters. I read it, along with other information when I took over this investigation. You didn't know it, but you were watched every step of your way by express men in the expectation that you would lead them to your father and the stolen money, if he was still alive. It wasn't exactly an express company responsibility that time, because the money had passed out of their hands, but we did it as a favor to the county authorities. They watched you in Denver and San Antonio and El Paso. The Rurales co-operated in Mexico. The American consul helped in Panama. It was there they quit keeping cases on you."

"Why did they quit?" Steve asked.

"Because they figured you had proved your point, which was that your father had never been in any of those places. That indicated, of course, that you were correct in believing Buck Santee had been murdered. However, there was no actual proof to back up that assumption until just lately, so the matter remained inactive."

Steve straightened. "Actual proof? What do you mean?"

"I'm now convinced beyond all doubt that your father was killed the night of the disappearance of the ten thousand dollars," Clum nodded.

"What convinced you?"

"The money he was accused of stealing has shown up."

"Shown up?" Steve demanded. "How do you know that?"

"That money could be identified," Clum said. "It was all in new twenty-dollar gold pieces—double-eagles—and was part of the only mintage in that denomination that had been turned out so far that year by the Denver mint. The coins bore the mint initial, of course. A small part of the mintage had gone to a Kansas City bank, where it was paid out to the Powderhorn Pool through the accounts of commission buyers. Cattlemen always like the feel of new gold money. The remainder of that mintage was shipped to St. Louis, where it went into the gold reserve of a bank, and was never placed in circulation at all."

Steve's voice was taut. "When did this money come to light?"

"About a month ago—although I only got word yesterday from headquarters. Someone there was slow to realize its significance in connection with my presence here."

"A month ago? You mean whoever had it waited three years to pass it off?"

Clum nodded. "Evidently they had learned it was money that could be identified. It's hang-rope money, you know. They thought three years was long enough. Even so, they went to great pains to avoid discovery. Nearly all of that ten thousand dollars appeared suddenly in Chicago. It was deposited in small amounts in different banks, and was withdrawn a day or two later. The withdrawals were taken in silver and banknotes. Because of the small amounts involved, no suspicion was aroused."

"Who——?" Steve began.

"I'm getting to that," Clum said. "Because of the three years' lapse of time several days passed before it was discovered that the Bugle robbery money was in circulation in Chicago. Federal agents traced out the manner in which it had been done. By that time the man who had made the deposits was long gone. Only one or two tellers could recall very vague descriptions of him. One said he had been an old man, bearded and heavily dressed, who seemed to be in bad health. The other gave a different description. Obviously the man was disguised."

"It could have been Buck Santee if he were still alive," Steve pointed out.

"But it wasn't," Clum said. "It was Louie Latzo."

Steve felt a fierce surge within him. "Latzo? Are you sure? How do you know that?"

"I didn't know that it was Louie until last night," Clum said. "I've always had a hunch Nick was back of these train robberies and I also figured he probably knew something about what happened to Buck Santee three years ago. But it was only a hunch until your fight with Louie and his pals. I arrived just as you and young Whipple were finishing them off. When Louie was knocked down I saw some objects fall from his coat pocket. He wasn't in condition to know that. After everyone had gone, I took a look. I found a nail file, a cigar case, and a pencil. Also a small notebook. This contained the names of quite a number of ladies. Some of these gals live here in Bugle. Some in Cheyenne. And two or three in Chicago."

"Chicago?"

"And there was something else relating to Chicago in the notebook," Clum said. "On an inner page, in very tiny writing, was a column of figures. Alongside each item was a street address. Also initials that I'm sure are abbreviations for the names of banks. In other words that was a check list of deposits that had been made in a dozen banks in and near Chicago. The column of figures totaled up to almost ten thousand dollars."

"You still have this notebook?" Steve asked.

"No. I didn't want Louie to know anyone had seen it. I copied the information, then returned the notebook, along with the other items, to where I had found them. Later I saw Louie come back and search around until he found them. He seemed very happy when he came across the notebook."

"But Louis wasn't in the Powderhorn at the time Dad was killed," Steve said. "Miss Maddox told me that he showed up in Bugle after I had left."

"He was acting only as his brother's agent in passing the money," Clum said. "Louie was a fool for keeping that book. I suppose it was because of the ladies' addresses that he stuck into it. It wouldn't the the first time that a man hung himself with a petticoat."

"I've always felt deep in my heart that Nick was the one," Steve said, and there was a savage, roweling fury in him. "I'll—"

"I'm asking you not to do a thing—at least until I give the word," Clum said urgently.

"Not do a thing?" Steve demanded.

"A wrong move now might spoil everything," Clum said. "That's why I came to you to tell you all this. Another reason is that I knew your Dad years ago. We wore law badges in a tough Kansas trail town when we were young men. We were close friends. Buck Santee backed me up a couple of times in some bad situations."

"But—"

"I'll see to it that, as far as the law is concerned, his name is cleared of all stigma as soon as I can write up my report and send it to headquarters."

"When will that be?" Steve demanded. "Hasn't this gone long enough? Three years."

"I'll take care of it as soon as possible," Clum said. "But I'm asking you not to go near Nick Latzo again. You might say or do something that would warn him. It's for your own sake as well as for the sake of recovering that money that was stolen last night along with what they got in the other two stick-ups. It amounts to close to a quarter of a million dollars in all."

"A quarter of a million? Is it true that Northern Express might not be able to pay off?"

Clum shook his head. "There isn't a chance. The express office won't open this morning. The men who are stockholders will be ruined. There are four or five of them and everything they own won't meet the loss at more than a few cents on the dollar. Some of the ranchers likely will go under also. Amos Whipple and his Center Fire are going to be hard hit, they say."

Clum added significantly, "Unless we can find that quarter of a million."

"Are you trying to tell me you believe all that money from the three robberies is still intact somewhere?"

"None of it has been spent to the best of our knowledge," Clum said. "Some of it was in bills which had recorded serial numbers. And a lot of the gold had come from the mint too and can be singled out, just like the money your Dad was packin' to the Spanish Flat schoolhouse that night."

Clum winked and added, "Leastwise that's the story that we put out right after the holdups started. It's true only to a certain extent, but they don't know that. But we're pretty sure it's being held, like Latzo held the other money, until they feel safe to either begin passing it or maybe until they figure they've got enough to skip the country with."

"You believe Latzo has it?" Steve asked.

"Who else? Your father's murder touched off a lot of things that have happened in the Powderhorn. At first it was only small holdups and burglaries. Cleanups stolen and paymasters robbed. Then the big stuff. Train robberies. It's only reasonable to figure Latzo and the shady crowd that hangs around his Silver Moon are back of it."

Steve stood gazing unseeingly at Frank Clum for a long time. "Do you know what this means to me?" he finally asked. "I've tried for three years to prove they were wrong about Buck Santee. Now you lay it right in my lap out of a blue sky. I'm grateful. I'll try to keep my hands off Latzo's throat until you say the word."

He went silent a moment, then said, "However, I've reason to believe that Latzo, even though he may have been back of what happened to Dad, probably had nothing to do with the train holdup last night."

"Not in person, of course," Clum said. "He was right in town. An ironbound alibi. But that don't mean——"

"I don't think he had anything to do with it at all," Steve said.

Clum hadn't expected that. Steve endured his searching inspection for seconds. "Want to tell me just what your reason is for saying that, Santee?" Clum asked.

"Have you talked to Amos Whipple about the holdup?" Steve asked.

Clum shook his head. "Should I?"

"If you do you'll probably learn that I'm suspected of having had a hand in it. Or guilty knowledge, at least."

Clum did not seem astonished. "I gathered it was something like that from Whipple's attitude last night," he said.

"And did you?"

Steve shrugged. "I landed at New Orleans from Panama only four days ago. Every minute of my time can be accounted for."

"Maybe you won't be given a chance to account for it," Clum warned. "Amos Whipple is workin' for Vigilante action."

"I know," Steve said.

Clum waited. When Steve offered nothing more, Clum walked to the table, picked up the torn envelope, and examined it. "Am I right in guessing that this was pushed under your door while you were asleep?" he asked.

"Yes," Steve said.

"I found one under my door also," Clum said. "Did your envelope have something like this inside it?"

He produced a leather wallet from the inner pocket of his coat and fished from it a hundred-dollar bill.

"Yeah," Steve said. "I've got its twin in my pocket."

They laid the banknotes side by side on the dresser.

"At least they took pains to see that this money couldn't be easily identified," Steve commented. "Both bills have been in circulation for some time—as much as bills of that size get around."

"It must be the opening move in some kind of a bribe,"

Clum decided. "It couldn't be anything else." He frowned. "Someone might have got onto the fact that I'm an express agent. That's what worries me. Aside from yourself I've confided in only one other person."

"I can savvy why they might try to bribe you," Steve said. "But why me?"

There was no answer. Clum produced a written note which had accompanied the bank bill. It was practically a duplicate of the one Steve had received.

"Someone has money to spend on the two of us for some reason or other," Clum said. "I reckon we'll learn in time who's tryin' to buy us off. We can guess, of course."

He tucked the banknote in his wallet and stored it back in his pocket. "I'll be happy to meet whoever sent it," he went on. "I suppose, if I follow instructions, I'll have that pleasure, sooner or later. I figure it'll be a mighty big help in the job I'm bein' paid to do."

He moved to the door and stood listening to make sure the way was clear. "I may have made a mistake in telling you my identity, Santee," he said. "But you have to take chances in this business. I pride myself on being a judge of men. I had great respect for your Dad. As long as I've gone this far I'll have to trust you completely. You understand, no doubt, that if these banknotes came from the men I'm after I might be in a dangerous position. They won't back off from murder if bribery fails."

"I understand," Steve said.

"It'd be as well that we remain strangers as far as other folks are concerned," Clum said. "But if you should have to get in touch with me and can't locate me personally you can probably get word as to my whereabouts from Burl Talley."

"Talley? You mean that he's the other man you mentioned as knowing you are an express agent?"

"I had to have some responsible person as a source of information about people in this range," Clum said. "Talley, being a leading citizen and widely acquainted, was the man. An intelligent person, Talley. Smart businessman. Everyone respects him."

Clum extended a hand, which Steve grasped. The man opened the door, made sure the hall was clear, then stepped out. Steve heard him walk away.

Steve stood thinking. Finally he followed Clum's example by carefully storing the banknote in the billfold which he carried. It seemed obvious, as Clum had decided, that this was a preliminary step in offering some kind of a bribe.

He knew Clum was still certain that Nick Latzo had been the brains back of the train robberies. Furthermore, he surmised that Clum was wondering why he had said that he doubted that Latzo had any part in at least the previous night's holdup.

Steve had no way of knowing about the other two train robberies. They may or may not have been engineered by Latzo. But it did not seem reasonable to believe that Doug Whipple would help Latzo or any of Latzo's outfit in a holdup, and a few hours later fight Louie Latzo and also back Steve's play against Nick himself.

In addition, Nick Latzo was guilty of, or deeply involved in the disappearance of Steve's father and the loss of the Pool money three years ago, as well as the murder of Henry Thane. If Doug was a member of any outlaw organization led by Nick, then he likely would have had an inkling of Nick's part in that crime.

That just didn't add up. Doug's nature was not the kind to tolerate murder or murderers—particularly of Buck Santee, who had been a kind of idol to him in boyhood. Train robbery might have appealed to Doug as a means of escape from boredom or as a chance to prove in his own mind that he was a swashbuckling, fearless individual who was strong enough to stand on his own feet. Lawlessness could be Doug's way of hurting his father for their differences.

The robbery of the Powderhorn Pool's own beef money might have appealed to Doug's sense of irony as a blow, not only at Amos, but at all others in the basin who looked down on him as a wastrel. But not murder.

Steve talked the chambermaid into bringing a tub and hot water to his room and he shaved and soaked away the grime of travel in peace, if not in comfort, for a wooden washtub was by no stretch of the imagination suited to the demands of his length.

In the midst of this operation a hand tapped the door. Eileen's voice spoke. "The hotel's on fire."

"That solves my problem," Steve said. "I'm wedged in this infernal contrivance. I'll die fast now at least."

"It sounded more to me like a buffalo was wallowing around in there," she said. "A fine time to be rising. It's midmorning. Have you had breakfast yet?"

"Not yet, but I'm willing."

"I'll order ham and eggs and flapjacks and if you don't show up in ten minutes I'll send Maggie, the chambermaid, with a bucket of ice water to dump on you."

"Make it steak and eggs," Steve called, untangling himself from the tub. "And I'll be there in five minutes."

She was awaiting him at the table in the dining room, which was nearly deserted at this off hour. She wore a divided riding skirt, half boots, and a cool blouse of blue and white polka dots. Her hair was brushed to a fine, dark red gloss. A straw hat of Spanish type hung on the back of her chair, along with a large handbag.

"Six minutes, exactly," she said. "You're either a man of your word or you're afraid of ice water."

"I'm both," he said. "And also hungry."

"And grouchy," she said. "You don't waste words, do you? How about saying good morning?"

"Good morning," he said. "Wait'll I get that steak under my belt. Then I'll have the strength to talk until you holler calf rope."

Through the nearby window they watched half a dozen returning possemen ride into town, swing up at the tie rail, and dismount. They came clumping into the hotel.

With them was Burl Talley. They evidently had been searching east of town and their morning ride had been fruitless. They were hungry now, and touched by the impatience of men who feel that they are wasting their time and yet are duty-bound to go through with the effort.

When Talley discovered Steve in Eileen's presence his tanned face went blank and stiff with an effort at masking his disapproval. Then he pushed that mood away and came walking over to their table.

"Morning, Santee," he said cordially enough. And to Eileen, "Breakfast at this hour, gal? You'll have to do better than that if you're going to be healthy, wealthy, and wise. So they tell me, at least."

"And they also say that you only get a worm for arising early," she said. "Now what would I want with a worm?"

"Steak, man-size and I want it cooked," Talley told the

64

waitress. "If I want raw meat I'll go out and shoot it myself. Say—what's this Santee has? Eggs! Great! Add a couple to that steak, smiling-side up, Dollie."

Talley laid his hand lightly on Eileen's. "You're staying in town a few days, I hope," he said.

"No," she said. "I'm riding out to Antler this afternoon."

"I'm disappointed," Talley said. "I wanted to be the fortunate man who would see you home, but I'm obligated to do my best in helping pick up the trail of the train robbers. Well, maybe I'll have better luck another day."

Talley rejoined the three men at the table on the opposite side of the room. He dropped his hat on a vacant chair and rolled a cigarette, then reached for the coffee that Dollie had brought.

Two of Talley's companions were riders, by their dress. The taller of the pair was a sinewy, leathery, gaunt-jawed cowboy of about forty. The other was younger and swarthy with the wide, square face and high cheekbones that spoke of Indian blood.

The third man had the garb and looks of a lumber-mill worker. He was a long-chinned individual with hair as dry and lifeless as dusty hay. All three wore pistols. Rifles were slung on the saddles of their horses in the street.

"The two punchers work for Burl at Rafter O," Eileen informed Steve. "Tex Creed, the older one, is foreman. The second one is known as Highriver. I never heard any other name for him. The third man is Whitey Bird, who is Burl's mill boss at the lumberyard."

All were strangers to Steve. In the past he had been well acquainted at the Rafter O and also at the planing mill. Evidently Talley had made some changes.

Steve was hungry, but preoccupied, as he tackled the steak and eggs. He saw Frank Clum stroll down the street, apparently without a care in the world.

Clum, glancing through the window, saw Talley and beckoned. Talley arose and walked outside and they stood on the sidewalk for a minute or two talking. Clum had his thumbs hooked in the armholes of his vest in the manner of a man discussing a business matter. Talley clapped Clum on the back and came back to his table.

Steve was thinking of Doug Whipple, wondering where he might be. Eileen's thoughts evidently were running in

65

the same path. She spoke softly, "It's no use for the two of us to pretend we don't know what the other saw last night."

He withheld his reponse for a time, wishing he did not have to answer. "Sometimes it's better to pretend," he said. "You always were good at it. Remember when you used to pretend that your dolls were grown-up people?"

"I was lonely then, even with my dolls," she said. "The only times I wasn't lonely after Mother and Dad went—went away was when I was with you and Doug."

"How about now?" he asked.

She didn't directly answer that. She gave him the measure of a smile. "We're all grown-up now, Steve, and we're dealing with real grown-up people, not dolls. It won't hurt to pretend—for a while at least. But, sooner or later, it must be faced."

She made a little gesture, dispelling these ghosts from her mind for the moment at least. "Are you planning on riding out to your place today?" she asked. "If so, we can go together. I left my horse at Sim Kendall's livery when I left for the convention. Shorty Barnes is in town. I saw him on the street from my window. You can borrow his horse. Shorty can catch a ride out to the ranch with a freighter later."

Steve pushed back his chair. He knew what she meant. Town was no place for him at the moment. "If Shorty won't mind. . . ." He nodded.

They arose. Burl Talley turned in his chair. "Leaving, Eileen?" he asked. "The schoolhouse party is off, of course, thanks to our train-robbing friends. However, as soon as possible, I'll get me a shave and a clean shirt and come galloping over to Antler with a box of candy under my arm."

He said to Steve, "I hope you find your house in shape, Santee."

Chapter
Eight

In the dining room Talley finished the food Dollie Lee placed before him. Through the window he watched Steve and Eileen walk down the street and enter Sim Kendall's livery.

Talley drank his coffee, lighted a cigar, and paid for the meal for himself and the three men. He arose and said, "I've some business I must look after. Don't wait for me."

From the Pioneer House he strolled down Bozeman Street to the office of his lumber business. This was where he could usually be found during the day when he was in town from the ranch.

He entered and locked himself in his inner office. He dialed the combination on a small safe, opened it, and from a locker drew a packet of bills of large denominations. He picked off four bills which were hundred-dollar banknotes, and returned the remainder to the safe.

He left the office, nodding to the elderly spinster who was his bookkeeper and said, "Jenny, I'll be back in an hour or less in case anyone wants to see me. I've decided not to ride posse any more today. Tomorrow, perhaps."

His horse still stood before the Pioneer House. En route in that direction he was buttonholed several times by citizens who wanted news about the train robbery.

He was passing the Powderhorn Security Bank when Charlie Hodges, its president, hurried from his office and called him in. Hodges, a balding, nervous man, was pale and shaking.

He led Talley inside his office and closed the door. "I've been informed by Pete Crain that Northern Express can't make good the beef money," he said. "They're stretched out so thin financially they'll have to go into bankruptcy."

"Well, it's not what you'd call a surprise," Talley said. "This merely makes it official. Everybody in town has been expecting it. Do you know what this means, Charlie?"

"I know," Hodges said wearily. "The ranchers in the Pool

are in deep trouble. That means that I'm in trouble too. The bank's fortunes are tied up with the ranches. We don't get much of the mining business."

"A bad situation," Talley said. "We've got to see to it that Bill Rawls catches these robbers. I'll build a fire under Bill when I see him, though I doubt that it's needed. He understands the situation."

"This might be seized out of Rawls' hands," Hodges said. "They're making Vigilante threats. They might even try to take it out on Pete Crain. He organized the express company. He's president and general manager. I told him to lay low."

"I can't say I'm happy about the situation myself," Talley said. "I had some six thousand dollars coming to me out of the Pool money. Maybe a little hang-rope medicine is what we need."

"Don't talk like that," Hodges protested. "That sort of thing can get out of hand. You can stand a loss. Others can't. You haven't got all your eggs in one basket."

"It's still my money," Talley said.

He left the bank, walked to his horse, mounted, and rode out of town. His three men came out of the Pioneer House a few minutes later, swung aboard their mounts, and also left Bugle to rejoin the manhunt.

Possemen were coming and going and all of the community was set on edge, for confirmation that the express company could not pay off was spreading swiftly.

The three men headed southward toward Art Stubbs' ranch, which was being used by the sheriff as the day's base of operations in that section of the basin, but Talley crossed the railroad tracks and followed the trail in the opposite direction up the basin toward the ford of the Powderhorn River.

Talley was alone on the trail. A few hundred yards before reaching the river he turned off the main route, passing beneath a massive archway of pine logs and jogged down a side road which curved through thick timber and brush.

After a quarter of a mile it opened into a clearing in which stood a rambling, ramshackle, shake-roofed structure. This was Nick Latzo's original gambling house, the Silver Moon.

Only the main entrance showed any attempt at glamour.

The weathered painting of a dancing girl adorned the false front. Above that arose the outline of a crescent moon which had been painted silver, but which was now considerably tarnished. Nevertheless, the tie rails bore the polish of constant use, and the clearing was beaten bare of all grass. The Silver Moon was a prosperous enterprise.

However, at this hot hour of noon the Silver Moon was nearly deserted. Not a single saddle horse was in sight. Talley dismounted and let the reins dangle, and walked through the doors and met the cool, echoing dimness of the main room.

A lone bartender was dealing a hand of solitaire as he sat on the lookout's stilt-legged chair. The roulette tables were covered and the faro layouts locked. The green curtain that served the small stage at the rear was lifted. An emaciated man wearing a derby and a woman with very golden hair, were practicing a soft-shoe routine on the bare stage while they kept time by humming a song. The roadhouse held the odor of stale beer, stale cigar smoke, and stale humans.

The bartender sluggishly left his seat and moved back of the polished counter. Then he recognized Talley. He was surprised. He straightened, and his manner became respectful.

"Beer," Talley said. "Is Nick up yet? I've got a little business deal to discuss with him."

"Nick's awake," the bartender nodded. "I had his breakfast sent into him half an hour ago. We don't see you here very often, Mr. Talley. I can't remember when——"

"Not often," Talley said. He picked up the glass of beer and walked down the echoing room and passed through a side door alongside the stage. He drained the glass and set it on a window ledge in the narrow passageway in which he stood.

This passageway carried him past half a dozen dressing-room doors. He reached the last portal, which, in contrast to the shabbiness of the others, was of heavy, varnished oak with a steel peek panel.

Talley knocked on the door and spoke loudly. "It's Burl Talley, Nick. I came to talk about that property on Bozeman Street you're interested in buying."

There was a growling response inside. Feminine footsteps

came hurrying. The panel opened and the round face of a girl with dyed red hair was framed there briefly. Then she freed the bolt on the main door and admitted him.

"Good morning," Talley said. "Even though it's afternoon to most people."

He eyed her with appreciation. She went by the name of Daisy O'Day, and she was a singer and dancer at the Silver Moon. She wore only a thin silk dressing gown over a lacy nightdress. She was buxom and attractive enough with sensuous blue eyes and full lips.

It was a large room with heavy furniture and garish velvet carpets. A bedroom opened to the left in which Talley glimpsed a silk-canopied bed.

Nick Latzo, wearing a flowered dressing gown and pajamas sat in an easy chair, a cigar in his mouth and the remains of a breakfast on the table before him. He had been totaling up the previous night's receipts and had pushed aside the coffee cups and dishes to make room for his ledgers and the stacks of silver and gold coins and packets of bills.

Talley discovered that another man was present. He had been hidden by the high back of a leather chair in which he was sprawled. It was Louie Latzo. He was fully dressed. He wore a patch over his left eye. His lips were puffed and discolored and he was suffering the bruises and the aching aftermath of his encounter with Steve.

"Morning, Nick," Talley said. "Good morning, Louie."

Nick Latzo's voice was surly and there was a wariness in him. "I figured you'd be ridin' hell-fer-leather with the posses, Talley," he said.

"The hills are full of posses," Talley said. "I'm not needed. I've changed my mind about selling that vacant land next to the Blue Moon to you, Nick."

"Land?" Latzo said a trifle blankly. Then he added swiftly, "Sure, sure."

"The train robbery left me in need of some ready cash, so I think we can come to terms," Talley said.

Latzo made a few notations in a ledger, swept all the money from the table into a leather handbag, and carried it as he arose and moved across the room. "Let's go into the office where we can talk it over and come down to cases," he said.

He led the way into a small room in which stood a heavy safe and a roll-top desk, and several chairs and a table. This room had no windows and was equipped with heavy double doors as a protection against both bullets and eavesdroppers.

"Keep your eyes off that girl," Latzo said after he had closed and bolted both doors. "I got money invested in her."

"And time?" Talley inquired.

"She's a good entertainer an' helps business," Latzo growled. "Don't go wheedlin' her into goin' with you on any of your trips to Chicago like you did with my last singer. That one never came back to Bugle either."

"I won't steal this one away from you, Nick," Talley said. "I have other plans."

"Are you crazy, comin' here in open daylight?" Latzo said. "What's wrong? Has anything happened?"

"You always were too excitable, Nick," Talley said. "Everything's under control. However this visit was necessary, for your sake at least."

"Fer my sake?"

Talley produced his wallet and extracted two of the hundred-dollar banknotes. He placed them on the desk in front of Latzo.

"There are two men in town who are each carrying a bill like these with them," he said. "They probably think it is a bribe of some kind. That's the impression I hoped to give them at least."

He helped himself to one of Latzo's cigars from a humidor and lighted it. "It isn't a bribe," he went on. "It's an incentive."

"What's that?" Latzo asked suspiciously. "What's this incentive?"

"You are to give these two bills to any persons you choose and tell them how they can double it," Talley said.

Latzo leaned back in the creaking swivel chair, a scowling distaste settling in his heavy face. "So that's it?" he said. "I might have knowed it'd be somethin' like that what brought you here."

Presently he asked, "Who are the two?"

"One of them goes by the name of John Drumm and is posing as a horse buyer," Talley said.

Latzo nodded. "I know the one you mean. He's been in the Blue Moon. Drinks a glass of bourbon an' bitteis, an' plays piker faro for a while, then leaves. He comes in often."

"But only when you are there," Talley said. "You should have noticed that. He's been keeping cases on you. His

71

real name is Frank Clum and he's working as special agent for the express companies."

Latzo uttered an oath and his scowl blackened. "Maybe he's keepin' cases on you too," he said.

"Not yet," Talley said. "But he is beginning to get too close to a lot of things."

"How do you know this?" Latzo demanded.

"Clum confided in me," Talley said. "He needed a source of reliable information and picked me for the role. That's the reward for building a reputation for integrity."

"How close is he?"

"Not close enough to move in—yet. But he will be eventually."

"An' the other man?"

"Steve Santee," Talley said. "He stumbled onto a piece of knowledge last night that might be embarrassing and also very dangerous to me. But more so to him. I believe he recognized one of my men during that little episode this side of Three Forks. There are reasons why he isn't too anxious to tell what he saw. He may never talk. But it's better to make sure that he won't."

Latzo tapped the banknotes scornfully with a thick finger. "You don't figger I'd be interested in piker money like that, do you, Burl?"

"Perhaps not. I can remember a time when you would be interested. In addition, you're growing too fat and soft for this sort of thing. But there are others."

Latzo smiled thinly. "Al Painter an' Chick Varney might hanker for that job at that, at least as fur as Santee is concerned," he said.

"And so would Louie," Talley said. "And get their heads in a noose. They'd be the first one suspected after that brawl they had with Santee. And you too. Santee made sure of that when he put you on notice at the Blue Moon last night. It was a smart play on his part. You've got to be smart too."

"But how——?"

"Keep Louie and his two pals away from Santee. It won't make any difference about Clum. Nobody knows there could be any connection. Amos Whipple and the ranchers are working themselves up to hang somebody. You don't want it to be your neck that's broken in a noose, do you? Or Louie's?"

"An' you don't want it to be yours, either, my friend,"

Latzo said. "We're in this together. Don't ever overlook that."

"I can't overlook it, unfortunately," Talley said.

Latzo was worried. "Plantin' them bills don't make sense. It's a circus stunt. Why did you do it?"

"My experience is that money talks," Talley said. "If your assistants are to double their profit they will have to make sure that they perform their tasks quietly so that they can search for and find their additional payment without being interrupted. Therefore they will be careful about the time and place so that they will be unobserved. That is highly desirable."

He turned toward the door, then paused in thought for a moment. "I'm afraid Douglas Whipple is too much of a burden to us also, to my regret," he said.

"Doug Whipple? You mean you want . . . ?"

Latzo let it trail off. Talley nodded. "He's a likable chap. But he has a conscience, unfortunately. He never fitted in with us. He went along the first time because he was drunk and in rebellion against life in general. Then he became so involved he could not quit us. He's been wondering ever since how to pull out."

"Involved is kind of a soft way of puttin' it," Latzo said ironically. "He's the one what touched off the dynamite that killed that Wells Fargo messenger on the Rock Springs job, wasn't he?"

Talley didn't answer. He produced his wallet, drew out the other two hundred-dollar notes, and tossed them on the desk. "It must be done," he said. "I've made up my mind. That's for Whipple. In his case I can't plant one of the bills on him for collection. He might suspect. So I'll give you the full amount—but it is to be paid only for value received."

"I still don't see any point in all this damned hanky-panky about plantin' money on people," Latzo said. "It might backfire."

"Maybe it's only my flair for the dramatic," Talley said. "And maybe, in case of this backfire, it might be helpful by confusing the situation."

"An' I don't see any sense in waitin' all these months to split up the money," Latzo said doggedly.

"You waited three years to pass off certain other funds that you had acquired by means I won't mention," Talley said.

"That was different. That was marked money."

"How do we know that some, or all of these other funds can't be traced also?" said Talley. "It's better to wait."

Latzo glowered, wanting to argue the matter further, but lacked the fiber. "I hope that wherever you've got the stuff hid out, it's safe," he growled.

Talley laughed. "Some day, Nick, I might even tell you where it's cached. You'll get your share, never fear. It'll be the easiest money you ever earned. Imagine getting paid for doing nothing."

"For bein' a sittin' duck, maybe," Latzo said.

"As for dividing it up, I'll decide the time and place," Talley said.

"Tex Creed an' the other boys might be a little hard to convince o' that if they really git the idea they want their divvy in a hurry," Latzo said. "They ain't the kind to set on their hands if they figger there's trouble comin'. They'll want to light out o' the Powderhorn mighty sudden."

"That bridge will be crossed if we ever come to it," Talley said. "Which I doubt. Meanwhile I would suggest that you do not let anyone know the subject of our conversation. By that I particularly mean your brother Louie. I don't trust him to be able to hold his tongue if pressure is brought to bear on him."

"Pressure? What do you mean pressure?"

"Use your head, Nick," Talley said. "You know, of course, that you are Clum's chief suspect in these train robberies. It is the natural viewpoint, because of the riffraff with which you consort, and I helped it along with a few veiled remarks, for that is exactly the situation we wanted to create. He is keeping close watch on you. He might decide to sweat someone. Louie, for instance."

"Maybe he's out there right now, watchin'," Latzo exclaimed. "Maybe he saw you come here."

"On the contrary he asked me to visit you," Talley said. "We had a conversation in the street this morning."

"What? He asked you to? What fer?"

"To snoop around and see if I noticed anything unusual, or if there were any strangers hanging around the Silver Moon. In other words he is letting me act as his assistant sleuth. I had mentioned to him a few days ago that you had approached me in regard to buying that vacant land next to the Blue Moon. I set that up as a genuine excuse for coming here."

Latzo sat troubled, his big, hairy fists clenched on the table before him. He finally drew a long breath and said, "We ought to take what we got an' quit. There's plenty fer the two of us, even after Creed an' the others are paid off."

"Nonsense!" Talley snapped. "It's too soon to get rid of that money. And there's bigger game in sight right now. I can own this whole damned basin before I'm finished. It's full of ripe plums. I'm in a position to start shaking the tree. Ranches can be picked up for a song before long."

"I ain't a cow raiser," Latzo said.

"You'll get your cut of the plum juice as well as what's in the cache," Talley said.

Latzo distrusted him, but seemed unable to do anything about it. In silence he unbarred the door.

Louie Latzo and Daisy O'Day were waiting in the larger room. For their benefit, Talley said heartily, "I'll think it over, Nick, and let you know. Four thousand is hardly enough. With the town booming that lot will be worth twice that much in a year or so."

He walked through the room, slapped Daisy O'Day on the hip, and laughed at Nick's black scowl and left the Silver Moon.

He rode into town. It was early afternoon and Bugle had settled into apathetic, heat-drenched exhaustion after the hours of sustained excitement.

Sheriff Bill Rawls came down the street on a tired horse, along with half a dozen other riders. Rawls' eyes were red-rimmed. He was mud-caked and needed a shave and sleep. He had the look of a harassed man who knew that much was expected of him and who also knew that he was beaten.

Among the sheriff's posse were Talley's two Rafter O cowboys, Tex Creed and Highriver.

Rawls, in response to Talley's questioning glance, shrugged and said resignedly, "Nothin', Burl. Not a damned thing. No trace of 'em. They flew off into thin air."

Talley spoke to his two riders. "Your pay at Rafter O goes right on as long as you want to keep looking for these men. You're under Bill's orders."

Talley rode on to his lumberyard. In his office he reached into a drawer and took a drink from a bottle of liquor. He sat for a time, thinking of Bill Rawls, riding stirrup to stirrup with two of the men who had helped hold up the train the previous night, and never suspecting. The other two members of the outlaw party had been Doug Whipple and Talley's planing mill boss, Whitey Bird.

He thought of his interview with Nick Latzo. He took another drink. He and Latzo had known each other nearly twenty years. As young men they had been members of a group of high graders and desperadoes that had operated in Colorado mining camps. They had used other names in those days.

Talley had served five years in Leavenworth Prison on a mail-theft charge. When he was released he had made an attempt to reform and achieve a respectable life. Chance had brought him to Powderhorn Basin and Bugle.

Nick Latzo had come into the Powderhorn also and had opened his Silver Moon near the ford. Slowly, inexorably they had drifted together again. The magnet and the needle. At first Latzo had been the magnet, Talley the needle. Now it was the other way around.

Talley had gained a dominating hold on Latzo when Buck Santee had disappeared with the Pool money. Talley had guessed that Latzo was responsible, for it had carried the earmarks of Latzo's methods in the past.

While the law was riding in circles, trying to find Buck Santee, Talley had trailed Latzo day and night and had caught him in the act of caching the stolen ten thousand dollars.

Latzo had admitted that he had murdered both Buck Santee and Henry Thane, and had hidden the former's body where it could never be found. That had not been Latzo's first experience with murder, but it had been his most profitable crime. Talley, although he had robbed and stolen, had avoided killing. The death of the Wells Fargo messenger in the dynamite blast had been his first close connection with the supreme crime.

Now he was forced into a position where, to protect himself, he was conniving the slaying of men. Once the acts were committed he was fully aware that his domination over Latzo would end. They would be on an equal footing. Such was the way he had drifted farther and farther from his long-ago intention of going straight.

Up to this time he and Latzo had served as very useful foils for each other. They had been careful never to associate openly. Thir meetings had been at night, in secret in Latzo's quarters. Publicly, Talley had let it be known that he did not consider Latzo a credit to the community. He discouraged his riders and mill hands from patronizing Latzo's establishments.

On the other hand, Latzo played his part by labeling Talley as a penny-pinching busybody who spent his life working on account books.

Tex Creed, Highriver, and Whitey Bird also were acquaintances from the past of both Latzo and Talley. Creed had been Talley's cellmate in prison. Whitey Bird and Highriver had known Latzo in the early days. It was Latzo who had sent them to Talley.

Talley had not taken part personally in the train holdups. Like Latzo, he had made sure he had an alibi to which many persons could attest. It was his strategy to continue, by innuendo, to point the finger of suspicion at Latzo by branding him as the brains back of the holdups.

This served to keep the law busy on a futile quest and to divert attention from himself. Not even Louie Latzo suspected that his burly older brother was serving as a decoy. Nick's reward for his role was to be a full share of the loot.

All of the money taken in the robberies was still intact under a troubled agreement that it would not be touched until such a time as the stake was big enough to support the lot of them in luxury. Then they were to go their separate ways.

The first train holdup had been carried out by only Creed, Highriver, and Bird. These three posed as peaceful, colorless men who drew their monthly pay from the Rafter O and the planing mill and blew it in on sprees and at the poker tables in Bugle.

But such thin numbers had nearly been disastrous. Creed, defying Talley's misgivings, had taken the hard-drinking wildling, Doug Whipple, along on the Rock Springs job.

That robbery was the one that had brought the full weight of the law into the chase, for Creed had used too heavy a charge of dynamite beneath the car in which an express messenger was holding out. The blast had ripped the car apart and had tossed the torn body of the messenger into the brush.

Doug Whipple believed he was the one who had touched

77

the match to the fuse that night. The truth was that he had been so benumbed by alcohol that he had taken little part in the holdup. It was Creed who had fired the fuse, but only Creed and Burl Talley knew that. Talley had seized the opportunity to hold a club over Doug Whipple's head by making him believe he was responsible for the messenger's death.

Talley shivered a little. What had happened to his resolve to go straight? First small robberies and holdups. Then the big money. Each crime, little or big, had been planned by him in every detail and rehearsed at the Rafter O.

With each success the urge for more and more easy money had grown. Avarice inspired increasing ruthlessness. Now, Talley, a little sick inside, knew there was no turning back. There must be more killings, and perhaps more, if he were to be safe.

He looked out and saw Amos Whipple ride past and dismount at the Pioneer House. Amos evidently had been on posse duty, for he was dusty and saddle-stiff. He was the person Talley had been hoping to see. He arose and left the office swiftly.

Amos saw him coming and waited. He laid a hand on Amos's arm. "You need something cold, Amos," he said. "They've got ice today, so the sign says."

They went into the barroom, which adjoined the eating room. It was dim and cool here. There were only two other drowsy patrons and these sat at tables.

Talley glanced around to make sure they were not being overheard. "Amos," he said. "I'm going to tell you something that I know won't go any farther. It was told to me in strictest confidence, but I've thought it over and believe it is too important to be the knowledge of only one person. Here it is. You may have met a man who calls himself John Drumm and represents himself as a horse buyer?"

"I know the man," Amos said.

"He's a federal marshal, detached from duty to work for the express companies, investigating these robberies," Talley said. "He told me his identity some time ago. This is what I wanted you to know particularly: Clum, which is his real name, Frank Clum, found an envelope under his door here at the Pioneer House this morning and it contained a hundred-dollar bill. There was a note in a disguised hand which stated that he would soon learn how to earn much more such money."

"I don't follow you," Amos said. "What——?"

"Clum thinks it's a bribe, of course," Talley said. "He told me about it as a precaution, however."

"Precaution?"

"It is evident that whoever sent that money is aware that he is an express agent. Perhaps this person will decide that if he can't buy Clum off he'll have to get rid of him by some other means."

Amos stared. "Rub him out, you mean? Did this Drumm, or Clum, say who he might suspect?"

Talley hesitated. "I don't believe I should repeat that. It was also in strict confidence. In addition Clum only suspects. He has no actual proof."

"But the man you're thinking about is Steve Santee," Amos said.

Talley shrugged. "I didn't say that."

Amos finished his drink. He said, "Thanks, Burl," and tramped woodenly out of the hotel.

Talley remained there a few minutes longer. He left the bar, walked into the lobby and down the hallway past the guest rooms on the lower floor as though he intended to leave the building by the rear exit.

Instead, he tapped softly on the door of the room that Frank Clum occupied. Clum had been awaiting him. He was quickly admitted. He declined Clum's invitation to sit down.

"Nothing to report, Frank," he said. "I talked to Latzo in his quarters. It's quite a place. I've never been inside it before. I used the sale of that vacant lot as an excuse. But I didn't see a thing that'd help you. I'm sorry."

"I hardly expected you to," Clum said. "But it was worth a try. It's the little things you pick up that usually solve the big ones. You saw nobody suspicious around?"

"Louie was with Nick," Talley said. "And a girl entertainer named O'Day. She seems to live with Nick. That was all."

He turned to go. "If I can be of any more help just give the word, Frank. This gang must be caught and caught soon. I'm still just as sure as you are that Latzo is back of it. There's nobody else capable of it to my knowledge."

He returned to his office at the lumberyard. There he spent

79

the remainder of the afternoon diligently working on accounts and discussing business matters with buyers.

At late afternoon he watched Amos Whipple ride out of town accompanied by two other ranchers. They looked grim and purposeful. They had the attitudes of men who had come to a stern decision.

Chapter
Nine

After they had left Burl Talley sitting in the Pioneer House dining room, eating his steak and eggs, Steve and Eileen walked to Sim Kendall's livery. Shorty Barnes' horse, a stalwart roan was quartered there along with Eileen's mouse-colored gelding.

Steve borrowed Shorty's saddle, rigged both animals and held the stirrup for her as she swung astride. She did not need that help, but she was pleased, and laughed down at him.

"My, but you've changed, now that old age is creeping on you," she said. "At least you no longer seem afraid of me. The last time you helped me on a horse you acted as though I was something you had to touch lightly and hold at arm's length. That was the day I graduated from the grammar grades at the Spanish Flat schoolhouse and your father forced you to escort me to and from the program."

"I remember," Steve said. "I had figured on going on a prospecting trip west of Cardinal Pass that day with Doug. I was a mite disappointed."

"I suppose I'm still facing the same kind of counterattractions," she said.

"Alongside of you a gold pan just doesn't seem to have a bit of allure," Steve said. "Not any more."

She laughed. "Now, there's a real compliment. In your travels you seem to have learned a few things about the opposite sex. At least how to flatter them."

She paused and gave him one of her slanting looks. "I wonder who taught you?" she added.

After this a soberness came upon them. They rode out of

town sedately and Steve was gripped by this knowledge of a new awareness of each other. She was conscious of it also. Suddenly she decided to end this trend of affairs. She slashed her hat down on the gelding's flank. "Last one to Spanish Flat is a chump!" she shouted.

They raced away from Bugle, across an open flat with the peaks of the Powderhorns towering to their right, hoary with the remnants of last winter's snows.

Steve stood in the stirrups and saluted the mountains again. "Here I am, home, rough heads," he said exultantly.

They sped into a stretch of timber and were berated by the driver of a jerkline freight outfit whose mules they threw into confusion as they thundered past. They skirted Long Ridge and crossed Blue Creek. Eileen's hair was flying and she was laughing.

Steve realized another rider had joined them in the gallop. He twisted in the saddle. It was Doug Whipple. He was mounted on a long-legged black. He must have emerged from the brush at Blue Creek.

He grinned at Steve and said, "If she beats us we'll duck her in the crick like we did the day she won those two big agate shooters that we were so proud of, at marble playing."

"You really mean it!" Eileen said. "And you'd do it, too."

She fanned the gelding ahead faster. Doug's black might have overtaken her, for it began to pull away from Steve's mount, but he caught Doug's saddle skirt and impeded it. "You're not leaving me behind, my bucko," he said.

Eileen beat them by a length to the door of the old frame-built schoolhouse. The building was locked and deserted, for the fall school term had not yet started. A few lengths of bunting blew in the wind over the door. The picnic benches and tables and the barbecue pit which would have been used on Pool Day stood forlornly deserted under the box elders. The benches and trees bore the carved initials of generations of pupils, including Steve's and Doug's and Eileen's.

Beyond the school building was Short Creek, a small, meandering tributary to the nearby Powderhorn River. Steve and Doug overtook Eileen, snatched her, screaming and kicking, from the saddle and carried her to the creek. There they ducked her face under water.

She arose gasping and hurled mud at them. She sank back, breathless and laughing on the grass at the brink of the stream, blowing water, and spreading out the wet strands of her hair to dry. She looked down at her blouse, which was soaked and clinging to her.

"I'm a sight, and it wasn't fair, and quit looking at me until I dry off, and I'll get square with the both of you when I get a chance," she panted.

She pulled Doug's hair until he yelled for mercy and filled her cupped hands with water from the icy stream and poured it down Doug's back.

Quieting at last, they lay side by side on their stomachs, gazing at the old schoolhouse. The only sound now was the rasping of locusts in the grass and the soft, liquid footsteps of the stream. The memories came back, poignantly sweet and also disturbingly bitter. Steve saw the bleakness return to Doug's face—and the regret. He watched the animation fade from Eileen, saw the shadows arise. The moment when they had captured the lightheartedness of their youth had escaped them again.

"Where did you drop from, Doug?" Steve asked.

"Just happened to be letting my horse take a drink when you two hellions went by like a stampede," Doug said.

Steve guessed that Doug had been waiting there at the ford for them—since morning perhaps. He was drawn out, gaunt. Steve guessed that he had drunk all night, and perhaps had not slept at all.

A reticence holding them, they mounted again and headed up the trail which carried them into greener and heavily timbered country along the river. The stream, brawling with the memory of its plunge down the canyons of the mountains, foamed and surged in youthful vigor as it swept through its rugged channel. Steve kept pulling up, gazing longingly at stretches of smooth water, picturing the trout that must be lying there.

"Save it for Black Rock," Eileen told him.

They rode onward and he tried to put out of his mind all recollection of that moment when he had seen Doug unmasked alongside the halted train. He glanced at Eileen and guessed that she too was trying to assure herself that it could never have really happened.

They topped the Canteen Creek divide and left the main road and angled down a wagon track through stately spruce and pines. Presently they came out in an open meadow in which a beaver-dammed stream meandered. They took a short cut across this meadow, avoiding marshes and leaping their horses across the stream, then climbed to a higher, firm grass flat. In this stood a solid, log-built, shake-roofed house, flanked by a pole corral which had a saddle shed as its wall nearest the house. There was a small old dugout nearby which had once been used as the residence before the house was built. The sod roof of the saddle shed and dugout were adorned by blooming lupine and Indian paintbrush.

This was home at last for Steve. The OK ranch. He pulled up, and Eileen and Doug halted at a distance behind him and sat watching him.

He said nothing. It wasn't necessary. He then led the way ahead to the house and dismounted before the door. Instead of the battened, weed-grown desertion he had anticipated, the building and surroundings presented a used, tended look.

"I did what I could," Doug spoke. "And Eileen came over regularly with a mop and soap."

He added. "You see, we figured you'd be back some day, Steve."

Steve opened the door and stepped into the house. He heard Eileen and Doug ride away, heading for Antler two miles farther up the creek.

The shadows of late afternoon lay in the living room, which still held the furnishings that were identified with his life. He ran his hand over the smooth, cold face of the iron heating stove. From its isinglass window it had cast the fascinating colors that had entertained him as a small child on so many wintry days. The rocker, and the clock on the wall with its china face and gilded hands were in their usual places. The clock's pendulum was motionless now, but he found the key in the blue glass vase on the mantle where his father had always kept it. He wound the clock and it began its soothing clucking.

He walked into the kitchen. Doug had stocked the cupboard with canned food and other supplies. The cookstove showed the benefit of use.

He stood remembering his mother in this place, and he remembered his father coming in from the corral after the day's riding to lift and kiss her lustily and swing her so that her skirts flew like a feather in the wind.

He could not hold off these memories nor their regrets. He walked outside and stood breathing fast with the effort of a man trying to break this surge of weakening emotions.

He was glad when Doug came riding back from Antler. They ate in silence the meal Doug cooked—a man's meal of fried beefsteak which he had brought back as a gift from Eileen, fried potatoes with onions, and baked soda biscuits and canned tomatoes. With coffee and canned peaches.

They sat in the twilight smoking, watching the horses graze on picket in the meadow. They turned the animals into the corral as early darkness came.

"I'd like to live two hundred years with everything just like it is here tonight," Doug said.

He got out his trout tackle, along with Steve's, which he had kept oiled and cared for, and they spent a pleasant hour debating the merits of flies and lures and natural bait, and recalling Homeric contests of the past with battling monarchs of the streams.

For in the morning they were going fishing, the three of them. They finally turned in for the night, carrying with them these memories of the past and the hopes for the morrow.

"We'll have elk steak as well as trout for supper tomorrow," Doug said. "Eileen says she's got an elk yard staked out up on Cardinal."

Steve started to drop instantly asleep. Then other memories returned . . . the train robbery . . . the black and hostile attitude of Amos Whipple . . . the fight with Louis Latzo . . . the mystery of the hundred-dollar banknote in his wallet.

And there was the confident, handsome face of Burl Talley smiling at Eileen. Sleep vanished. He lay awake with these phantoms. He realized that Doug also was beleaguered and torn by his own thoughts.

He suddenly aroused, aware of the sound of approaching horses. He rose to an elbow. He heard Doug sit up.

Riders were turning off the main road and coming up to the house. He arose and peered from a window. All he could see was an indistinct group of mounted men. They pulled up in front of the house.

A voice shouted, "Light a lamp, Santee, an' show yourself. We aim to search your house an' ask a few questions."

It was the heavy, dominating voice of Amos Whipple. Steve stood debating it a moment, a deep and molten

84

opposition in him. Doug spoke softly. "If you want to run them out of here I'll back your play, Steve. They're on the prod and want a victim. They don't care who that victim is."

"That's your own father out there, Doug," Steve said. "Stay out of this."

He lifted his voice and said, "All right. Wait'll I get into my pants."

He lighted the lamp and dressed. He buckled on his six-shooter. Doug, a queer, sardonic glint in his face as though he was bracing himself for chastisement, did not bother to arise from his bunk. He sat there, bare to the waist, his wide, freckled shoulders clear of the covers, waiting.

Steve opened the door. With a groan of leather and the tramp of boots Amos Whipple dismounted and led four men into the lamplight. They were armed with six-shooters and rifles. They glared at Steve, challenging him to try to question their right to be here.

He knew all of Amos's followers. They too had once been friends of his father. Now they were beset by the knowledge of loss and the fear of ruin and by anger and frustration. They were men ready to take the law into their own hands.

Amos paused in stride when he saw his son sitting on the bunk. "You should not be here, Douglas," he said sadly. "There should be a limit to the shame you heap on me."

"I've lived in this house quite a lot for the past three years, Dad," Doug said. "It's been almost like home to me. Almost, I said. There's nothing like a real home. Fact is, this house always seemed like home even when I was a button."

Amos felt the sting of this, Steve noted, but decided not to pursue the subject. He went rummaging through the house, poking beneath the beds with the muzzle of his rifle, pushing aside curtains, peering into corners and cupboards and tapping the floor in search of hiding places.

He did find the trap door leading to an opening, and for a time there was excitement as this was investigated. But it proved to be only the root cellar, long unused.

The presence of his son had taken the wind out of Amos's sails. He was unable to maintain the determination that had brought him here.

He abruptly motioned his companions to leave and followed them to the door. Turning, he said, "Coming, Douglas?"

Doug shook his head. "Leave this to the law, Dad. You don't know what you're monkeying with."

His father gave him a withering look. He glared at Steve, started to say something, but decided against it. He turned and walked out into the darkness.

Steve listened to the receding sounds as they rode away. He knew that Doug's presence had stayed off a showdown between himself and Amos and his Vigilantes. A violent showdown, perhaps. Undoubtedly, they had meant to make him explain why he had jostled Amos's arm during the train robbery. One of them had carried a coiled rope under his arm. A rope with the many folds of a hangman's knot as the hondo. He had been marked for Vigilante trial. He was to have been persuaded to talk with a noose around his neck.

"They were of a mind to hang you," Doug said. "Why?"

"If they were they decided against it," Steve said.

Doug stared unseeingly at the door through which they had gone. "You know about me, don't you, Steve?" he asked suddenly. "Me and the holdup?"

Steve had felt that this was coming and had been trying to find a way to meet it. Now that he had to answer, he still did not know what was best.

Finally he said tersely, "Yes."

"Eileen too?" Doug asked.

Steve nodded and waited.

"How long have you known?" Doug asked.

"Since the night of the holdup," Steve said. "Your mask had snagged on a tree limb, which lifted it off just at the time someone opened the firebox in the engine."

"Yeah," Doug said. "I was scared when it happened. But I was beginning to think nobody had seen."

"You were lucky, in a way," Steve said. "Only Eileen and myself happened to be looking in the right direction at that moment."

"But something else must have happened," Doug said. "My father seems to think you had a hand in the holdup. "Why is that?"

"Maybe he's suspicious of anyone named Santee," Steve said.

Doug shook his head. "It's more than that. Amos has his faults, but he wouldn't go so far as to try to hang you just for being Buck Santee's son. He must have reason to suspect you."

"He's probably only trying to scare me," Steve said.

86

"I know him better than that," Doug said. "He never tries to run a bluff. He's an unforgiving man in matters of right and wrong. He convicted and sentenced your father after the Pool money disappeared three years ago. He had been Buck Santee's friend, but that didn't count, once he had pronounced his judgment."

Doug quit talking for a time, then said slowly, as though apologizing for his father. "But he was pushed into it. He's honest almost to a fault. He can't see the flaws in others. He can be led by a glib tongue."

"Who led him?" Steve asked.

"I'm not sure," Doug admitted. "But I'm beginning to understand a lot of things that've happened. Amos fired a shot at someone during the holdup. It's my guess that you did something to upset his aim, or he might have shot one of the outlaws down. Me?"

"It's past and done," Steve said.

Doug showed a twisted smile. "Amos used to say that blood is thicker than water when he was accusing you of having helped Buck Santee get away with that beef money. He and I are father and son. Nothing can change that. Beneath his stiff-necked pride Amos loves me. I know that. I also know what it would have done to him if he had shot that outlaw and then learned that he had killed his own son."

Steve said nothing. Doug spoke again. "And I know what it would have done to my mother. She still believes I'll come home to Center Fire some day and that everything will be as it was before."

He again gave Steve that fragment of a smile. "You've squared for that day on the ledge when we were boys, a hundred times over, Steve. I don't count, but for saving Mother —and Amos too, from heartbreak the other night, I thank you."

"You know one reason why I came back to the Powderhorn, Doug?" Steve said.

"Two reasons," Doug said.

Steve eyed him questioningly. When Doug did not elaborate, he went on, "I intend to run down the man who killed my father and Henry Thane. I know Dad was murdered."

"You've learned something?" Doug asked.

Steve nodded. "Yes. But I can't pass it along right now. I'm going to see that the guilty man is hung for it. If any others were mixed up in it they'll also go on my list. The law might not see it my way. Then I'll tear a page from Amos's book and take justice in my own hands."

"That sounds like a warning," Doug said.

"I've got a question that you can answer, or not, just as you choose, Doug," Steve said. "Here it is, cold. Was Nick Latzo or any of his crowd mixed up in the train stick-up?"

"Latzo? I've fallen pretty low. I've helped rob my own father, my own friends. But I draw the line somewhere, Steve. Would I have helped you against that slimy little Louie and those other two if I had been hooked up with a cutthroat like Nick?"

The next question was obvious. Just who was Doug hooked up with, if not Latzo? But it was one Steve did not ask. He felt that it would not be answered.

"Doug," he said. "Get out of the Powderhorn before it's too late. There are forces working against you that you don't know about. Get out while you can. That's all I can tell you."

"How does a man get stuck in the mire this way?" Doug said exhaustedly.

"It's never too late to wade out," Steve said.

"I don't expect you to believe this, even though it's true," Doug said. "But I didn't know I was going to rob my own father and the other ranchers. I didn't know they were aboard that train. I thought they were still in Cheyenne."

"But they *were* aboard," Steve said.

"I know it doesn't change things," Doug said. "But I've got to talk to somebody. I was told it was a shipment of money to the bank. I had been drunk as usual. For a week. Maybe I didn't do any real thinking. Maybe I didn't want to think. But I sobered up in a hurry when I learned I'd robbed men I've known from boyhood. And then I found out I'd stolen money from you, too."

"How did you get started in this sort of thing?" Steve asked.

"I was drunk that time too," Doug said, his voice flat and neutral as though he was discussing a stranger. "It was months ago. One night I found myself wearing a mask and riding with—with other masked men and helping rob a train. They told me I was the one who lighted the fuse that killed an express messenger who refused to surrender. I had too much alcohol in me to remember anything clearly. I guess I did it. It makes no difference anyway. I was a member of the

88

gang. They won't let me forget about that messenger. They hold it over me."

"Who are 'they,' Doug?" Steve demanded.

There was no reply. He hadn't expected one. And he asked no more questions.

He barred the door, laid his pistol within reach alongside the bunk, and marked the location of Doug's rifle so that he could get to it in the dark in a hurry if the need came. He snuffed the lamp.

He lay a long time and knew that Doug was not asleep either. He listened to the clock ticking on the mantle and tried to find an answer for many things.

"I'll see to it that you get your money back," Doug spoke.

"It's the Pool's money," Steve said. "See that they get it back."

Finally he fell asleep. At intervals he would awaken and start up, reaching for the pistol. Then he would sink back, listening to the silence, realizing that what had aroused him was only the stirring of the wind in the timber. For the night passed and Amos Whipple did not return.

Chapter
Ten

A rider jogged into the yard before dawn and Steve came out of the bunk with a rush and stood with the six-shooter in his hand, thumb on the hammer.

But it was Eileen's voice that called lightly. "You, there in the warm beds. It's almost daybreak and if you're going to eat elk steak and trout today you've got to face the facts of life. Let me in. I'm shivering like a quakie tree. It's frosty this morning."

Steve fumbled for his clothes, got into them and lighted a lamp. He admitted her.

It wasn't until then that he discovered that the bunk in which Doug had been sleeping was empty—the blanket and quilts thrown back.

He looked blankly at Eileen and walked outside to the corral. Doug's horse and saddle were gone.

89

"I thought I slept light," he said. "But he injuned away without arousing me."

"Why would he do that?" she asked. "He was looking forward to going with us."

Steve avoided answering that, banging the stove lids around as he built a fire. She huddled over the stove while it warmed. She had her hair stuffed into a wide-brimmed hat and wore a turtle-neck sweater and a duck saddle-jacket and riding jeans cuffed high on her half boots.

She had brought a slab of bacon and a jar of wild honey. She shed jacket and sweater as warmth pervaded the kitchen, and pushed Steve aside to take over the cooking.

She forced herself to be gay and chipper at first, but she was aware of Steve's silence and became more and more subdued. A pinch of worry formed above the bridge of her nose.

She placed a platter of hotcakes and crisp bacon on the table, along with a pitcher of warmed honey, and seated herself opposite him.

"Exactly what happened last night?" she demanded.

"Happened?"

She leaned across the table, pushing her face closer to his. "Don't try to hold out on me, my lad, or I'll twist your ears like a corkscrew. Where did Doug go? And why?"

"I don't know," Steve said. "Out of the country, I hope."

"Out of the country? Then something did happen!"

"Some ranchers came by early in the evening and searched the house," he said.

"Ranchers? Oh! Uncle Amos?"

"He was with them," Steve said. "In fact he seemed to be the ramrod. They searched the place. They found nothing. They left. That's all there was to it."

"What—what did they expect to find?" she asked wanly.

"They didn't say," Steve said. "The money from the train robbery, maybe."

"Or more likely they intended to try to force you to talk," she said. "Amos knows you jostled his arm deliberately. Was Doug here when they came?"

"He was here," Steve said.

"What happened between him and his father?"

"Amos was considerably upset," Steve said. "It spoiled his plans. I believe it saved me from a session that might have become very rough."

Eileen was silent for a time. "Steve," she finally said. "I

know how you feel about Doug. But this isn't fair to you. You can't take the blame for——"

"A man gave me some valuable information about my father's death yesterday," Steve said. "In return for that he asked me to say nothing and do nothing until he gave the word. He is an express company agent. You will not mention this to anyone."

"And—and you say Doug has left the country. You warned him?"

"I only hope he's gone," Steve said. "I don't know for sure. All I know is that I remember a day when I was hanging above Racehorse Rapids and——"

"I know," she sighed. "I was there. You can't forget a debt. But you can't pay for it with your own life. And Uncle Amos and the others aren't in a mood to listen to reason. They're facing ruin. Men like that strike out blindly."

Steve leaned over suddenly, took her in his arms, and kissed her. She burst into tears. "Damn it!" she sobbed. "Why did we have to grow up? Why couldn't we just have gone on as we did, playing together, fishing, hunting, and——"

"It's going to be just like it was for today at least, for you and me," he said. "And I'd be in a hell of a stew right now if you hadn't grown up. Come on! How about that elk you talked about? And that lunker in Black Rock?"

She dabbed at her eyes. She looked at him through the mist, then kissed him softly, tenderly.

"It's a deal," she said. "Steve, three years is a long time to wait. I—I don't want to lose you now."

She clung to him for a time, kissed him again, then moved back. "There's something I want to show you today," she said. "It's across the river, high up on Cardinal. That's elk country up there too. I stumbled on this thing a week or so ago. We can hit Black Rock toward sundown on the way back and that's when that big trout is most likely to be hungry."

Steve saddled, pocketed a fly book, and packed reels and sandwiches into saddlebags and tied rods across the cantle. Eileen had a .44-.40 rifle in the boot on her saddle. She led the way.

They crossed the meadow, forded Canteen Creek, and struck directly westward across a timbered rise for the river. Pink dawn was overhead now, but the frost lay white and pure as new snow on the grass and deadfalls. Night's heavy shadows still fought the oncoming day in the thick depths of the lodgepole pines.

They rode in silence, the air crisp and exhilarating in their throats. The glow of dawn presently reached through the foliage and touched them. All the shadows on their minds were driven away and they lived only for the moment.

Cattle huddled in the timber. Some wore Eileen's Antler brand. Others were Amos's Center Fires and Steve spotted a few of Burl Talley's Rafter O steers. This was open range.

"There'll be OK cattle here soon, I hope," he said. "I'm going to restore the brand."

They crested the rise, with the horses beginning to steam, and dropped downward into the rough and wild valley where the Powderhorn River began its long sweep northeastward through the basin. The sun was now striking the high peaks above them. Cardinal, the tallest, wore ermine and gold.

Half an hour of steady riding brought them to the river where it foamed and thundered over a boulder-studded course. They followed its margin upstream and presently climbed above its surface, skirting the rim of the stretch of gorge known as Racehorse Rapids.

Steve dismounted and walked to the rim at one point and gazed down the sheer drop to the rapids. This was where Doug had saved his life. Eileen watched and said nothing as he stood there for a time.

He mounted and they rode onward. They reached quieter water above the gorge and forded the river at a wide, sandy crossing where the horses blew complainingly as the icy water touched their bellies.

Beyond the river they began the climb up the flank of Cardinal Mountain. This was slanting country in all directions and clumped with aspen and coniferous timber and spangled with green parks and clearings.

Grazing horses drifted out of their path. There were not many cattle west of the river, for this was used principally as range for saddle stock by all of the outfits in the upper basin. Many of the horses bore the girth marks of recent work. They were from the remudas that had taken part in the beef gather and were turned out now to rest and fatten.

They mounted higher. A six-point buck, shaggy and wild-eyed, broke from cover and went tearing through the brush out of sight.

Twice Steve saw the fresh tracks of shod hooves. Once,

from beyond the river, came the faint report of a signal shot. Posses were still riding in their hunt for the train bandits, a search that was growing increasingly vain with the passing of time.

Hooves grated on rock higher up and two men appeared from around a clump of aspen on a ridge ahead. They were Burl Talley's two riders, Tex Creed and Highriver.

Both made quick motions toward their holsters. They paused, then sat motionless and Steve had the impression they were tautly waiting his next move.

Eileen lifted her voice. "Hello there! You're getting jumpy! Did you think you had bumped into your holdup men?"

The pair stirred their horses and descended the slant to meet them. "Didn't recognize you in britches, Miss Maddox," Creed said. "We been ridin' posse so long we're gittin' bug-eyed. We didn't expect to meet anybody up here. Ed Walters an' a puncher from Center Fire are supposed to be workin' along east o' the river toward the ford. Did you see 'em?"

"No," Eileen said. "We're out to bag an elk I've got staked out higher up—I hope. We're going to fish the river this afternoon."

"You'll have better luck with elk lower down," Creed said. "We sighted a nice bull this side o' the river awhile ago. Quite aways off just this side o' that old avalanche scar."

"Thanks," Eileen said. "We'll take a look."

"Good huntin'!" Creed said. "An' fishin'." He lifted his hat to Eileen, Highriver did likewise. They nodded to Steve and rode on past. They had the gaunt, drawn aspect of men who had been too long in the saddle.

"We're about ready to call it quits," Creed spoke back to them. "We're goin' on into town after we report to Ed. Whoever stuck up that train are likely a long ways from the Powderhorn. It's my guess they never came in this direction."

The two men rode on down the slope and were presently lost to sight among timber and ridges.

Eileen took the lead again and she and Steve sidehilled the mountain. They were paralleling the river now, but well above it. All of Powderhorn Basin was spread below them, stretching in a wrinkled carpet of somber green and saffron hues. The river was a strewn ribbon which coiled through the rough country, glittering here and there in the sun, the rays of which were now striking downward into the basin. Bugle was hidden in the distance by an arm of Long Ridge.

They were at nine-thousand-feet elevation now, with big timber below them and timberline showing on a naked mountainside to their right where a rockslide reflected the sunlight. The air here had a brittle quality and was so clear that Steve plainly saw a marmot's head jut above a rock on the rockslide, although the distance was a long rifleshot away.

The animal's shrill whistle came faintly. That was followed by a louder sound, and it wasn't the marmot. It was the whistle of a bull elk and fairly close at hand.

"All right," Eileen whispered, and her eyes were bright with excitement. "He's there—just where I expected him to be."

They dismounted, leaving the horses tied to ground pine. Eileen pulled the rifle from the boot and thrust it into his hand. They moved a step at a time up a rise.

Nearing the skyline, they crawled on hands and knees, careful not to displace rock. Steve could hear Eileen breathing in high suspense. Their shoulders touched and she moved close, her lips touching his cheek. "Welcome home, Steve," she said. "Welcome back to all the things you like to do."

They made the last few yards to the rim on their stomachs. Steve peered cautiously, and Eileen assayed a look.

A stately bull elk grazed in a shallow, sizeable draw where a small stream supported aspen and a growth of grass. The place was sheltered from the wind by rocky ridges and warmed by the radiation of the sunlight. Farther across the draw were three cow elk with calves and in the distance were more.

It was an easy shot. Steve estimated the distance and centered the sight on his quarry. But he could not squeeze the trigger. He lowered the rifle and gave Eileen a wry look.

He tried again. And again he could not fire. "This is no good," he said. "For three years I've been dreaming about this, and now I can't bring myself to knock over that noble creature as though I was slaughtering a steer for beef."

He arose into plain view and shouted. The elk whirled, hair ruffled. In the next instant it was off with all the power and speed of its wild nature.

He raised the rifle, followed his quarry a moment in the sights, and let drive. The elk kept going, vanishing into quaking aspen over the ridge southward. The remainder of the band was gone also, crashing away through the aspen.

He lowered the gun and looked guiltily at Eileen. She began to laugh. "Don't try to tell me it was buck fever," she said. "You missed him deliberately." She added, "I'm glad. It just isn't a day for destroying beauty—or illusions."

"It looks like we eat trout or nothing," Steve said. "That shot likely spooked every elk on this side of the mountain. You can bet I won't be in a mood to miss by the time we hit Black Rock pool."

"Remember that I said I had something up here I wanted to show you," she said. "It isn't far. It's something that has puzzled me."

They returned to the horses and she led the way for another mile or more along the flank of the mountain. She dismounted and said, "Here it is."

They were in a small draw which faded out into a great thicket of willows, ground pine, and aspen. A game trail led into this tangle. Steve followed her into this opening on foot. Paths such as this had a habit of dwindling out, leaving a man with the alternative of turning back or trying to fight his way ahead an unknown distance through heavy vegetation.

But Steve noticed that horses had used this game trail —both shod and unshod animals.

The brush extended to the base of a low clay bluff. Abruptly the trail widened and Steve found himself gazing at a man-made habitation. It was a dugout, almost a cave, in fact, for it was backed into the base of the bluff where a natural alcove had been enlarged and closed in with rude walls of ax-cut lengths of lodgepole pine and aspen.

Dead brush and branches had been heaped against the face of the structure to mask its presence. A casual intruder might have passed it without discovering it.

"I stumbled on this about a week ago," Eileen explained. "That was after the beef gather had been shipped. I helped Shorty shove the spare saddle stock across the river into pasture. Some of the horses which had been here all summer had taken it into their heads to hide up high, and I rode up here to push them down nearer the river. Two of them took off down this game trail, and that's when I found this hide-out. I had a feeling that the two horses had been here before. They seemed to know this dugout. I left for Cheyenne the next day and had nearly forgotten about this thing."

Steve moved aside dead brush to get at a crude door hung on leather straps. He opened this portal and stepped inside. There was no sign that the place had ever been used as a shelter for men, but it had been occupied by saddle stock recently. Within the past hour or two, by the fresh tracks and sign. Two sacks of grain stood nearby and one had been partly used.

It was not a line camp, for such duty was unnecessary west of the river. The towering Powderhorns were sufficient protection from drift in that direction.

Steve gazed around, a cold excitement forming in him. "You used the right word," he said to Eileen. "Hide-out."

This dugout was outlaw handiwork. This was a relay point where fresh horses were spotted before a robbery for emergency use in escaping over the mountains in case something went wrong and it was necessary to flee the country ahead of pursuers.

He studied the interior and decided that four horses had been quartered in the structure for perhaps three days. The animals had just recently been released, and the dead brush had been carefully replaced across the front of the structure.

Palpably it had not been necessary to use the relay horses and there had no longer been need of holding them ready. The law had never come that close to picking up the scent of the men who had staged the train robbery. For there was no question but that this relay station was a part of that affair, at least in Steve's mind.

He looked at Eileen and saw that she was beginning to understand all these things. A somber shadow lay upon her. He knew she was thinking of Doug.

She turned abruptly and headed for the open. She walked faster and faster until she was running back down the game trail as though pursued by evil.

Steve carefully replaced the dead brush over the face of the hide-out and followed her. They mounted in silence and headed toward the river. Neither mentioned what they had discovered in the thicket.

Halfway down the mountain, four riders came spurring out of timber into view ahead. One was Ed Walters, first deputy sheriff under Bill Rawls. With him were Tex Creed and Highriver and a cowpuncher who worked for Amos Whipple.

"Was it you folks that done the shootin' awhile ago higher up?" Walters demanded as he rode up.

Steve nodded. "I cut loose on an elk. Missed."

The deputy was disgruntled. He was a ruddy, heavy irascible man. "A hell of a time to sling lead in these parts," he complained. "You cost us two miles' ride up this damned slant on footsore hawses."

"My fault," Steve said. "But we had passed Creed and this other rider here on our way up and told them we were after elk. We took it for granted you'd know it was us who did the shooting."

"You didn't tell me that, Tex," Walters said, aggrieved.

"It slipped my mind," Creed said. "An' we'd have had to make sure they hadn't bumped into these train robbers, no matter what." He turned on Steve. "Did you sight anything up there outside of elk?"

"Nothing worth shooting at," Steve said.

Ed Walters eyed Eileen sourly. "You all right, Miss Maddox?" he asked.

"Why shouldn't I be all right?" Eileen asked, bristling.

Walters didn't reply to that. He gave Steve a critical look, turned, and led his posse away. "This is the last place they'd have come to," he was grumbling. "Bill Rawls would never have sent us on a wild goose chase west of the river if you hadn't put him up to it, Tex."

Steve and Eileen followed at a distance, but their trails soon parted, and the posse headed for the ford downstream. They picked their own trail directly down the mountain toward Black Rock pool.

The pool was a fine stretch of clear water where the river swept past an upthrusting ridge of bedrock that was black with the constant spray. This created a wide inshore eddy. In the depths of this deep hole were boulders and waterlogged driftwood where big trout lurked.

They ate their sandwiches, boiled a pot of coffee and then lay dozing in the sun-warmed sand alongside the river until the afternoon shadows reached the stream. They then set up their rods and after a long debate, during which Steve refused to take precedence, they compromised by agreeing to cast simultaneously.

Steve watched Eileen as she stripped line and danced the fly above water, working for distance. She picked a whorl forty feet from shore as her target. She had laid aside the sweater and jacket and was in a checkered blouse and was barefoot, her jeans rolled high. She waded into the margin of the stream.

Steve fought the urge to walk to her, take her in his arms, and tell her all the things he had been wanting to say to her almost since that first moment aboard the train. He found in him a fear of unutterable loss—a desperate fear.

He moved to the stream playing the rod. He judged his time and placed his own fly on the surface at a likely spot at the same moment Eileen let her own lure settle to the water.

Almost instantly there were violent eruptions around the dancing objects. Eileen uttered a cry of delight. Steve experienced the electric excitement of a hookup as he straightened line.

They had fish, but not the monsters they had anticipated. Eileen's trout, when she finally beached it, proved to be a thirteen-inch beauty. Steve's catch was only slightly smaller.

They cast again, but nothing arose. They fished for half an hour longer and Black Rock pool lay sullenly unresponsive. Now and then Steve saw great shadows move in the depths. But none of the big trout would rise.

Somehow the zest had gone. In fact it had vanished at the moment they had stood in the dugout on the mountain and had comprehended its significance. Since then they had been maintaining only a pretense of the lightheartedness with which they had set out at dawn.

Sundown came. They saddled up and rode toward the ford. A cold wind drove down from the peaks. Abruptly the weather changed. Rain clouds came rolling over the rims.

It began to rain and they donned slickers. The downpour increased, slatting through the timber, funneling in streams from their hatbrims, finding its way down their necks.

It was dreary nightfall when the lights of Eileen's ranch appeared. Shorty Barnes' widowed sister, who acted as housekeeper at Antler, came to the door, peering and called, "I was worryin' about you, Eileen."

Steve drew the saddle from her gelding, turned the animal into the corral, and carried the rigging into the shed. She stood with him there in the shadows and kissed him. "Whatever is going to become of Doug?" she said tiredly. "And of you, Steve? Please be careful."

She seemed reluctant to part with him, but finally turned away and walked to the house. She stood in the doorway, watching as he rode away.

His own ranch was dark and forlorn in the rain. He cared for the horse and fled from the storm into the house. Lighting the lamp, he got a fire going and cooked a supper from the remainder of the steak and other food.

He ate and afterwards sat with a mug of coffee in his hand, trying to decide his course. He was gripped by complete frustration, unable to make a move in the matter of his father's death, because of the promise he had made to Frank Clum, and he was equally handicapped in the matter of the money he had lost, because of Doug's involvement in the robbery.

He added pitch fuel to the stove and it roared busily, casting flickering bands of light in the kitchen. The storm rumbled through the tops of the timber. Heavier gusts of rain beat on the roof, and the drip of water was a soothing undertone.

He thought of Eileen, remembering her as she had stood at Black Rock pool. He thought of her steadfast loyalty and of her grief over Doug. Burl Talley's face came into focus in his mental picture, serene and confident. That brought a cold desolation in him. It was as though he was seeing Eileen's true future.

He became aware of a vague scraping sound. Absently he decided that it might be a squirrel at a window. In the next moment he aroused, knowing there would be no squirrels out at this time of night and in this weather.

That saved his life. There was a shadowy something at the window. It was the head and shoulders of a man who wore a black slicker buttoned to his chin and had a neckerchief pulled over the lower half of his face. Only his eyes were tangible beneath the brim of his rain-sogged hat.

The man had a six-shooter in his hand and it was pointed. Steve hurled himself aside as the weapon exploded. Glass burst in a shower, the fragments striking him and tinkling against the stove and on the floor.

Chapter
Eleven

He felt the vicious, pushing thrust of a bullet at his arm. It was as though some arrogant hand had tried to grasp him. It whirled him, overbalancing him, and he fell.

He twisted around, scrambling with legs and arms, and drawing himself toward the wall beneath the window. It was an instinctive maneuver for self-preservation, because that area was a difficult point for the assassin to command through the broken glass of the small opening.

As he moved the roar of gunfire beat at him, and the room was alight and quivering with the explosions of a six-shooter which was being emptied at him in a frantic attempt to pin him to the floor with bullets.

He did not know if he had been hit. He felt nothing, for the only thought in him was to try to stay alive until he could reach his own .45, which he had hung on a peg not far from the window.

He made it to the wall. The crash of the gunfire ended and he heard a hammer fall on an empty. He pulled himself along the wall, gazing upward at the opening above him. The concussions had blown out the lamp and only the dull flicker from the stove lighted the room.

He expected a second gun to be pushed through the window and to face bullets that would finish him.

This did not come. He got to his knees, and his hand found his holster where it dangled on the wall. He snatched out the pistol and sent a bullet angling through the opening. The flash lighted the window and he saw that it was vacant. The masked man had backed away.

He raced to the door, tore it open, and leaped out, crouching low and diving aside. No shot came.

He stood braced there in the darkness, searching the night for sound or movement. The rain began soaking him to the skin. He felt a burning pain along his left upper arm, but the arm was unimpaired and he believed it had been only a graze.

The first slug that had twisted him around seemed to have done no physical damage. He discovered that the bullet had torn through the heavy fold of his shirt sleeve, which he had rolled above his elbows while cooking.

He restrained his breathing, listening. The only sound for a space of time was the drone of the wind in the timber and the rain drip from the eaves of the house.

On a hunch he went plunging straight ahead, with a noisy stamping of his boots in the muddy ranch yard. He had guessed that the assassin must be crouching near. His maneuver panicked the man into revealing his whereabouts. A six-shooter exploded twice from the vicinity of the saddle shed. The man had managed to reload.

Steve was not hit. He heard one of the bullets grind into the wall of the house at his side. He fired back once, but knew that he was only wasting powder, for he could hear the other breaking into running escape.

He fired again into the air, hoping the flash would reveal his opponent. He gained only a glimpse of a figure darting around the corner of the saddle shed.

Steve raced in the opposite direction around the corral, circling it. He had the advantage of knowledge of the terrain. He also had the advantage of initiative and impetus.

It was certain that the man would have a saddle horse nearby. The natural point at which the mount would have been tied, and the easiest to locate in the darkness, would be the opposite end of the corral, for that was far enough from the house so that the sound of the approach of a rider would have been covered by the wind and rain.

He almost collided with the man's horse, which was tethered to the pole rails of the corral just about where he had estimated that it would be.

The horse reared. At the same instant he realized that his man was coming up at a run from around the opposite side of the corral. He ducked past the plunging horse, risking a blow from a hoof, and crashed bodily into his opponent in the darkness.

The man fired his pistol, but Steve had anticipated that and had flailed out with both arms in a sweeping motion. His left wrist struck the other's gun arm an instant before the weapon flamed and the bullet went into the sky.

His fingers grasped the folds of a slicker. His own pistol was clear. But the other's gunhand was free also. Steve had no choice, for he knew that in the next instant a bullet would tear through him. He jammed his gun against the slicker and fired twice.

The sledging force of the .45 slugs tore the man from him. He heard a terrible, choking sound. His own forward motion was still carrying him and he fell over the man who was going down at his feet.

A gun flashed almost beneath him, but the bullet went into the mud. A voice, drowned now in both blood and despair, said thickly. "Don't shoot me again, Santee. I'm—done—fo——"

That ended it. The last shot had been fired by the man in the final reflex of expiring life.

Steve crouched there for a time, the fingers of his left hand still locked in the slicker of the figure that lay unseen beside him in the blackness and the rain. His foot rested on the other's gun-arm. But there was no longer any harm in the assassin.

He got to his feet at last and walked shakily to the house and lighted the lamp in the kitchen. He did not replace the chimney, but carried the glass base, with its flaring and smoking wick turned up, shielding it as best he could from the storm.

He bent over the sprawled figure, peering in the wavering light. The hat and the handkerchief mask had fallen aside.

The features that looked up at him were those of a stranger. He stood there for some time, peering incredulously. His first thought had been that the assassin had made a mistake in picking him as his target. But he remembered that the man had uttered his name before he died. There had been no mistake.

The lampwick guttered out. He carried it to the house and relighted it. He examined his own wound. It was a bullet scrape just beneath his armpit. A painful injury which was bleeding, but was not much more than a deep scratch. He tore a clean shirt into strips and formed a bandage.

He carried the lamp to the saddle shed and left it there while he walked to the far side of the corral with a blanket. He wrapped this around the limp form and lifted its weight in his arms, and carried it to the shed. He laid the body on the lid of the six-foot-long feedbox which his father had built years in the past for the storage of bran and corn for the saddle stock.

He moved the lamp closer. The dead man was tough-featured and marked by hard drinking. He wore cowboots, run-down at the heel, but otherwise, neither his shabby garb nor his general appearance was that of one who spent much time working cattle.

He had carried only the one six-shooter and its action now was choked with mud. Steve searched the pockets for some means of identification. He placed the results on a bench. A plug of tobacco, an elk-tooth charm, two brass checks of the kind that could be won in slot machines and were good for drinks at bars. These particular ones, according to their inscriptions, were cashable only at the places operated by Nick Latzo.

Steve found himself shaking. The aftermath of that moment of supreme effort when he had fought for his life, hand-to-hand, with this stranger in darkness, was hard upon him. He had to drive himself to go ahead with the grisly task of ransacking the pockets of a corpse.

The inner pocket of the coat yielded a partly punched meal ticket issued by a Front Street restaurant and half a dozen coins in small change. Also a thin packet of bills, held by a paper clip. The bills seemed to be of small denominations.

But no! Steve picked up one of the folded banknotes. It was a hundred-dollar bill—a twin of the one he had in his own wallet, and of the one Frank Clum had shown him. It bore a stain of dark blood which was already drying.

He stared. The probable real purpose of these banknotes occurred to him. He and Clum might have been too quick in jumping to the conclusion that they had been meant as a mere bribe. The person who had requested that they carry the bills on their persons could have used that method of making their murder worth while to a paid killer. The shoddy form on the feedbox had all the appearance of a man whose fee for assassination would not have been high.

A new thought startled him. "Clum!" he said aloud. "They might be after him too!"

He debated it an instant. He placed the bloodstained bill in his pocket and raced to the house to get his coat and slicker. He got the saddle out of the shed, blew out the lamp, and closed the door, dropping the wooden peg into the hasp.

Moving fast, he rigged the horse and mounted. He hesitated a moment, gazing at the dark outline of the shed, regretting the necessity of leaving even the body of a person who had tried to murder him alone and unwatched.

He rode away toward Bugle. He still had Shorty Barnes' horse, and the animal was equal to the task in spite of the day's journey on the mountain.

It was past ten o'clock by the clock in the window of Eli Morton's jewelry store when he rode down Bozeman Street on the tired horse. The rain had slackened to a thin drizzle. The street was muddy and desolate. The conservative section of town was turning in for the night, but the gambling houses were doing business, though even there the weather had subdued the activity.

The front of the Pioneer House was still lighted. Steve dismounted at the rail, looped the reins, and walked into the lobby. The clerk was disappearing upstairs on some errand, a bundle of towels over his arm.

Except for a sleepy, round-stomached man who had the appearance of a clothing drummer, the chairs in the lobby were vacant.

Steve walked down the hall. This passageway had a runner of faded red carpet down its length and was lighted only by a single ceiling lamp.

Someone was just leaving by way of the rear door. It was a man's figure. The light was too dim for positive identification, but Steve had the impression that it was Louie Latzo. The door closed behind the departee.

Steve's step quickened. He did not realize that he was a hard-looking figure. His face still bore the marks of his fight with Louie and the two roughs. His dark beard had grown during the day, giving his features a thin, wild cast. His shirt, stained with his own blood and that of the man who had tried to kill him, was visible beneath his open slicker, which he had unfrogged so that he would have access to his holster. He was streaked with mud as a result of his struggle at the corral. More mud had spattered him during the ride to town.

He remembered that Clum's room had been three doors from the one he had occupied. He hardly counted on finding the man in his quarters, but it at least offered a starting point in the hunt he expected to have to make.

However, lamplight showed beneath the door. He stood a moment at the portal, listening. From another room half a dozen doors away came voices. Someone was entertaining visitors over a convivial bottle. A door slammed on the upper floor. He heard the clerk descending the creaking stairs at the front, en route back to the desk. There were other sounds in the building—normal sounds.

Frank Clum's room was silent. Some warning of disaster impelled Steve to draw his six-shooter.

He tapped on the door. The silence was unbroken. He tapped again, harder.

The door swung slightly ajar. It was not locked, and had been only partly caught on the latch.

Steve pushed it open. Frank Clum was at home. He sat slumped forward, his head resting face-down on a small table that served as a writing desk. A bottle of ink was spilled, the black stream still dripping over the edge of the table to the brown carpet.

There it was joined by another stain. This one was blood. The handle of a knife jutted from Frank Clum's back.

Steve moved numbly into the room and to the side of the slumped figure. Clum had been writing a letter. Steve mechanically read the words:

> To My Dearest Wife:
> I am writing this in my room at . . .

Frank Clum had died as he had started that message to his loved one. A knife had been driven into his back and into his heart. The top of his head had been caved in by a violent blow. He had been blackjacked to make sure of the job.

Clum's coat was on the floor, the pockets turned inside out. His wallet lay nearby. Steve picked up the wallet. It was empty. The hundred-dollar bill was gone.

Steve grasped the handle of the knife in the instinctive, humane attempt to free it from human flesh. It was a wooden-handled, cheap affair of the kind that could be bought in any outfitting store. It did not easily yield and he realized that removing it was useless anyway, and that it should be left where it was until the law was called in.

Before his fingers relaxed from the handle a woman's shrill scream of terror brought him around, startled.

He was looking into the horrified face of a gray-haired woman who wore the apron of a chambermaid and carried a broom. She was the night maid who had passed by the open door, and had looked in.

She screamed again with all the frenzied strength of complete fear. She dropped the broom and fled, still screeching at the top of her lungs.

Doors opened and confusion began. Guests poured into the hall from other rooms. A man appeared in the door staring. It was the plump man who had been drowsing in the lobby. Others joined him.

Steve gazed at them. He realized he still had his six-shooter in his hand. He holstered it. "Come in here, you," he said, pointing at the drummer. "And you," he added, singling out another. "The rest of you stay out. Someone send for the marshal."

The two men he had indicated did not move. Nor did the others. The hall was filling with new arrivals. Those in the rear were babbling questions. "That man just killed another one in the room there," someone was saying hoarsely. "The maid saw it. He used a knife. Stabbed him in the back."

In the lobby the chambermaid was still screaming hysterically.

"I didn't kill him," Steve said. "I just happened by."

He was remembering the dim figure he had seen leaving by the rear exit, the one that might have been Louie Latzo.

He tried to push past. "Let me by," he said. "I saw someone go out by the back door just as I came down the hall. Maybe he's the one who killed this man."

Nobody moved. Nobody yielded an inch. They merely stood looking at him. "You better stay here," the drummer said. The man lifted his voice. "Fetch the marshal! Tell him there's been a murder."

Steve drew his .45. "You fools!" he said. "The real killer is getting away. Stand aside."

They saw the grimness in his eyes and gave way suddenly. The drummer's face was chalky. He backed away hastily, forcing those behind him to yield.

Steve gave them an additional shove and raced through them and down the hall to the rear door. It opened into a deserted back street. The rain had settled in again and he ran along this dark, muddy thoroughfare, peering in both directions. No one was in sight. There were many paths between buildings by which the figure he sought could have reached other streets. Behind him men were spilling from the Pioneer House. Someone shouted, "There he is!"

Another touched off a pistol, firing three times with the wildness of an excited, frightened man. Steve heard a bullet strike a building and another ricochet from stone.

He called, "Hold your fire! You've got it all wrong!"

He backed into the shelter of a building corner. Other shots were fired. Men were spreading out in the street and shouting to each other.

A deeper, authoritative voice arose. "Come out of there, whoever you are, with your hands up."

That was Marshal Mart Lowery, who had arrived.

"Tell those idiots to quit shooting, Lowery," Steve said. "I was only chasing the murderer. I'm coming out."

He expected to be shot down by some overwrought person. He holstered his gun and walked toward the dark mass of men.

Mart Lowery's figure detached itself from the group and loomed before him. "Well, well!" Lowery grunted, peering at him. "Steve Santee! You know, I felt in my bones you'd be mixed up in this."

Before he was aware of the officer's intention he felt hard metal close around his left wrist. He was handcuffed to the marshal. An instant later his right hand was similarly linked to another man who wore a deputy's shield. His six-shooter was taken from its holster.

"Why did you knife that man?" Lowery demanded.

"Clum was already dead when I found him," Steve said. "Listen to me! I think I know who killed him. Take off these damned handcuffs. Use your head, Lowery!"

"Clum, you say," Lowery said. "I understood the man's name was Drumm—John Drumm. What did you do? Kill the wrong man?"

Steve went wild. He yanked Lowery toward him and tried to swing a fist, forgetting that his arm was manacled to the deputy. Even so the power of his effort carried that officer with him and into the marshal. The three of them went floundering down in a heap in the mud.

Lowery, panting, rose to a knee. "You need coolin' down!" he said, and brought the long muzzle of his six-shooter smashing down on Steve's head.

Chapter
Twelve

Steve's next memory was of throbbing, heavy agony in his head. Through the haze that seemed to cloud his vision he made out blurred faces. Gradually his sight cleared, and his thoughts focused. They had carried him to the jail and he was stretched on a bunk in a cell.

Tobias Skelly, the wizened medic who had doctored the ills of the Powderhorn people for years, was rolling down his starched cuffs. "He'll be all right," Tobias was saying. "He escaped a fracture, thanks to having a hard skull. Mart, you ought to be more careful when you buffalo a man. You might have killed him."

"It'd have saved the county the cost of a trial," Lowery said.

The doctor left. Another man remained in the cell with the marshal. Steve groggily recognized him. It was Burl Talley.

Steve finally managed to sit up. The cell kept whirling around him, and he clung to the bunk. Slowly that vertigo faded, slowly all memory came back—Frank Clum's body with the knife in the back—the futile pursuit of that furtive figure—and the handcuffs on his own wrists.

And his own fight to the death at his ranch with the stranger. That aroused him and his hand sped to the inner pocket of his coat where he had been carrying his wallet. During the ride to town he had placed in it for safekeeping, along with the original banknote, the blood-stained hundred-dollar bill he had found on the assassin.

The wallet was gone. "Lookin' for somethin'?" Lowery asked ironically.

"Yes," he said. "My wallet."

"The one in which you put the hundred-dollar bill that you took from Frank Clum?"

Steve looked from the marshal to Burl Talley. The latter's lean face was grave. He shook his head and said, "You might as well tell Mart all about it, Steve. I'm sorry. Sorry for you."

Steve pulled himself to his feet with an effort. Tobias

Skelly had added a band of court plaster to his other relics of combat. It ran from his temple on up into his hair, where a patch had been shaved out. This covered the gash where Lowery's gun muzzle had broken the skin.

He steadied. He had been at a disadvantage sitting down. He was as tall as the lanky marshal and an inch taller than Talley.

Lowery sensed this opposition in him and moved back a pace. "Don't try nothin', Santee," he warned. "I've stood enough o' your roughness."

"So you know that his name was Frank Clum?" Steve asked.

Lowery nodded. "I've learned some things lately. I know now that Clum wasn't a horse buyer. He was sent here by the express companies. He was tryin' to run down the train robbers."

He added, "That's why you killed him."

"On the contrary I went there to prevent just what happened," Steve said. "I was too late. I sighted a man leaving by way of the door to the back street as I came into the hall from the lobby. He had made his getaway by the time I got out there."

Lowery grinned derisively. "Got a story all fixed up in a hurry, didn't you? But it'll take plenty more than that. How about the two hundred-dollar bills we found in your wallet? We know Clum was carryin' one. An' we know how he got it."

"Neither of those two bills were taken from Clum," Steve said. "I was sent one of them at the same time Clum got one. I——"

"Sure," Lowery jeered. "Sure you got one. That was half payment for killin' Clum. The other half you got from his wallet. Clum's blood was on it. The blood from where you knifed him. You didn't know about the blood did you? Now let's see you explain that away."

"It isn't Clum's blood," Steve said. "It was the blood of a man who tried to kill me at the OK tonight. I shot him. His body is in the saddle shed at my place. I found a hundred-dollar bill in his pocket."

Lowery stared and his jeering grin widened. "How's that? Say, you must have been awake longer than we knew about to have dreamed up a yarn like that. What kind o' a sandy are you tryin'——"

Steve turned to Burl Talley. "I know you must be the

109

one who told Lowery about Clum. How do I know that? Because Clum told me he had taken you into his confidence. We two were the only ones in the Powderhorn who knew Clum's real identity."

Talley shrugged. "It's true Clum confided in me. He told me only yesterday morning that someone apparently was trying to bribe him. He said he had received a hundred-dollar bill, along with a note hinting that more money would be easy to earn if he was agreeable. But it seems now that it was part payment for killing him."

"He told you about talking to me, of course?" Steve asked. "And about finding the same thing under my door?"

"He did mention your name to me, but not in any such connection," Talley said reluctantly. "As a matter of fact he was inclined to believe you were in league with those train robbers."

Steve stared disbelievingly. "That's impossible!" he exclaimed. "Why, Clum told me——"

"Frankly, Santee," Talley said. "I must warn you that you're in a very serious situation. It would be better if you made a clean breast of everything."

Steve had the sensation of wading upstream against a current that grew increasingly powerful and that, sooner or later, would sweep him away. "Listen to me!" he said. He forced himself to speak slowly, carefully. He related his talk with Clum.

"Clum had turned up some new evidence in the disappearance of my father which might spoil a lot of work by the law if I told it now," he said.

"I'm sure, if there actually was any such new evidence in regard to your father you'd be better off telling it to Mart here and now," Talley said.

"It would be still better if I talked to express company agents first," Steve said.

Talley shrugged. "What's this story you were telling about killing a man at your place tonight?"

Steve recounted the details of his escape from assassination and of his fight to the death with the stranger and of finding the blood-stained banknote in the dead man's possession.

"You were right about it being payment for murder," he said to Talley. "I realized it also. Apparently someone wanted both Clum and myself put out of the way. Why?

Maybe that someone was afraid we might learn too much about a lot of things in addition to the murder of my father."

Mart Lowery, who had been listening impatiently, said, "Bosh! I ain't got time to listen to any such pack o' lies."

"Be fair, Mart," Talley remonstrated. "Santee's story should be easy to corroborate or disprove. You can send someone out to his ranch to take a look at this dead man—if one is there."

"That's county territory," Lowery said. "It's the sheriff's responsibility. I don't aim to go to the expense o' sendin' a man on a wild goose chase twenty miles on a night like this. I'll turn it over to Bill Rawls as soon as he shows up."

Talley turned to leave. "I'd advise that you retain a good lawyer, Santee. I'm afraid you're going to need all the help you can get. I know that Eileen Maddox feels obligated to you because of childhood association. For her sake I'll do what I can. I'll try to get in touch with Carter Benton and have him talk to you tonight, late as it is. Carter's the smartest lawyer in these parts."

"I don't need a lawyer," Steve said. "I'll be out of here by morning."

"I hope so," Talley said, and walked out of the cell and down the stone floor of the jail out of the cellroom. He had the attitude of a man who had shown Christian tolerance in a trying situation and who was now glad to wash his hands of the affair.

Mart Lowery followed him. The iron door swung shut behind them and the lock grated into place. A bleary-eyed, ragged saddle tramp who occupied the opposite cell on a charge of drunkenness, peered scornfully and spat on the floor. "Gittin' so a man finds hisself in the damnedest company in these here jails," the man said. "I don't go fer knifin' in the back. They ought to hang you higher'n a buzzard's nest."

Steve found himself breathing hard. He had heard of men who went berserk under confinement and had battered themselves to death against the bars like wild animals. He could understand this now.

Time passed. The jail was used jointly by both the county and the town officers. The marshal and his deputies shared the office space at the front with the sheriff's staff, with mercy a partition between the two sections.

There was no sign that anyone knew or cared whether

Steve was dead or alive. Finally the night turnkey came into the jail room from the office, swinging a bull's-eye lantern with which he made the rounds of the cells. He flashed the light through the bars, scrutinizing Steve from head to foot.

"Where's Lowery?" Steve demanded.

"Lowery? Home o' course. In bed fer an hour or more by this time. Where'd you think he'd be at this time of night?"

"Did they send someone out to my place?"

"To your place? Do you mean to hunt that ghost you was yarnin' about?"

"Damn you, did anyone go?"

The turnkey scowled. "Keep a polite tongue in your head, Santee. Or maybe you'd like me to git a bucket of cold water an' chill you down. Ever sleep in a bunk that's soppin' wet?"

"I asked you a question," Steve said grimly.

"Mart notified the sheriff's office," the turnkey said sourly. "But Rawls is asleep an' wasn't to be disturbed. Bill's been ridin' quite a fur piece an' deserves some rest. I reckon someone'll go out there in the morning. That'll be time enough." The man laughed. "Yore dead man won't up an' walk away, now will he?"

Steve turned away. The turnkey guffawed again and left the cell room, extinguishing the single oil lamp that had given light, leaving the place in darkness—a darkness that Steve could feel reaching deep inside him.

The saddle tramp began to snore. Other prisoners slept noisily also. Steve stretched out on the bunk. He lay rigid and awake. He found himself sweating, although the damp chill of the night had crept into the place.

He finally dropped off for an hour or two, but awakened when dawn seeped into the dismal room. He walked the cell, trying to force the numb cold out of his marrow—and out of his heart.

Daylight strengthened. He could hear the stirring of the awakening town. A jerkline team ground past the jail down Bozeman Street, dragging a loaded wagon and trailer by the sounds. Other outfits moved out, bound for the mines. Wheels rumbled and bit chains jangled.

A steam whistle blew. That would be the working signal at Burl Talley's planing mill at the head of the street. Six-thirty.

Steve had already been in the cell a lifetime. His head still ached from the blow Lowery had struck. He gave way to his futile rage and rattled the iron door.

It was a long time before the door from the office opened. It was the day turnkey who had come on duty. "What in hell do you want?" the man demanded. "Tim told me that you likely would try to stir up trouble. Keep quiet. You'll git some breakfast when I git good an' ready to fetch it."

The door closed again. An hour passed. The turnkey came in with a plate of flapjacks and a mug of coffee which he had carried from a restaurant. He thrust the food through the small panel in the cell door and started to turn away without a word.

"I want to talk to Lowery," Steve demanded. "Is he on duty yet?"

"It's Bill Rawls you'll deal with from now on," the man said. "You're a county prisoner. County's payin' for your board now."

Then he left. The coffee was cold, the flapjacks soggy. Midmorning passed. Noon approached. Nothing happened. Merely the passage of time. One long minute after another. The hands on Steve's watch seemed frozen. Occasionally he called out and rattled the door. It brought no response.

An unpalatable noon meal was brought by the same turnkey who refused to answer his questions.

It was midafternoon when Sheriff Rawls came striding into the jail room, followed by Mart Lowery and Carter Benton, the lawyer.

Rawls was a big, gaunt, high-shouldered man with a thin, arched nose. An honest, but unimaginative man, he had been sheriff of Powderhorn County for half a dozen terms. He was fresh-shaven and dressed in clean garb, but his eyes were still tired and the marks of strain were on him.

"Hello, Santee," he said, and his tone was strictly neutral. He jerked a thumb toward the lawyer. "I reckon you know Mr. Carter Benton, of course? Burl Talley asked Carter if he'd consider defending you."

"I agreed to discuss it with you, at least, Santee," the lawyer said. He was a crisp and starchy man of sixty with a clipped gray mustache and wooly, iron gray hair. He was prosperous and wore an expensive business suit.

"Anything you say can be used against you," Rawls warned

113

Steve. "But you might also be able to help yourself if you cooperated with the law."

"Don't say a word, Santee," Carter Benton spoke. "Not until you and I have had a chance to talk in private."

"I've already told it all," Steve said. "Sheriff, did you send out to my place to find that fellow's body who tried to kill me last night?"

"Surely, you don't aim to try to stick to that story?" Rawls said testily.

"You mean you haven't bothered to send anyone?" Steve demanded angrily.

"I did, to my regret," Rawls said. "I sent Ed Walters out there this morning to take a look."

Steve gazed at him. "And he didn't find anything?" he said slowly, for he had seen the answer in Rawls' face.

"There was no corpse in your saddle shed or anywhere else," Rawls said. "What did you gain by tellin' a windy like that?"

Somehow, Steve had expected something like that. It was the way the current was running resistlessly against him.

"Bloodstains!" he said. "There must have been some stains on the lid of the feedbox. That's where I laid him after I carried him in from the corral."

Rawls shook his head. "Ed said he looked the place over. Nary a speck o' blood. I don't recollect him mentionin' this feedbox, but I take it that he examined it too."

"Tracks! There must have been tracks around!"

"Plenty," Rawls said. "Horse tracks, boot tracks. An' all blurred by rain so they didn't mean a thing."

"And the broken window in the house," Steve said hoarsely. "The man emptied his gun at me through that window. There'll be bullet holes in the kitchen. The broken glass will show . . ."

He quit talking, silenced by the sheriff's expression.

"There ain't much of a house left," Rawls said slowly. "You had visitors last night. They're the ones what made all the tracks I mentioned. Your house burned out inside durin' the night. There's nothin' left but some rain-soaked log walls. The saddle shed wasn't touched."

Steve was ashen, sick at heart. Amos Whipple and his Vigilantes evidently had carried out their threat, and had returned to his ranch. He could see that Rawls believed this.

114

And it was also plain that Rawls had no intention of doing anything about it.

In fact, he sensed that the sheriff approved of what had been done and was relieved that some of the burden of punishing the will o' the wisps he had been unable to pin down was being taken out of his hands, even though by illegal means.

But that did not explain the disappearance of the stranger's body. It did not seem reasonable to believe that the ranchers would have removed the corpse without at least letting Rawls know.

A new arrival came rushing into the cell room. "Steve!" It was Eileen. She wore mud-flecked riding garb and a quirt still dangled from her wrist. Evidently she had just leaped from the saddle at the jail door.

She pushed past Rawls and grasped both of Steve's hands through the bars. "I just heard about it!" she said. "I couldn't get here any faster."

"You shouldn't have come at all, Miss Eileen," Rawls said. "I don't like to be rough, but Santee was caught red-handed, knifin' an express detective in the back. There's good reason to believe he's tied up with these men who've been robbin' trains. I figure you ought to know the cold truth. Don't let your sympathy get away with you."

"Bosh!" Eileen snapped. "You're all wall-eyed idiots. What's all this about knifing a detective?"

Rawls shrugged and withdrew from the jail room, taking Mart Lowery with him.

Carter Benton cleared his throat. He patted Eileen on the shoulder. "Santee will want to talk this over with me, my dear," he said. "He's due for arraignment shortly, and if I agree to defend him, I must have time to prepare a plea. Perhaps you would prefer to wait in my office."

"Stay here," Steve said to her. "I want you to hear every word."

Step by step he went over the story while Carter Benton listened and asked questions. He omitted two items, however. One was Doug Whipple's part in the train holdup.

Carter Benton seized upon that point. "It's common knowledge that you prevented Amos Whipple from shooting one of the outlaws," he said. "Is that the truth? If so, why?"

"Let's just continue to say that I jostled Amos's arm accidentally," Steve said.

Benton frowned. "It is not my custom to defend a client who withholds facts from me. Let's hope you change your mind before we go to trial. It may be the only means of saving you from the gallows—if there actually is any hope."

"You believe Steve is guilty, don't you?" Eileen demanded.

The lawyer only smiled dryly and prepared to leave. "Coming, my dear?" he asked.

"Not at the moment," she said. She remained with Steve.

The second item that Steve had withheld from the lawyer was Frank Clum's revelation linking the Latzos with the Pool money his father was accused of having stolen.

He told all of this now to Eileen, keeping his voice down on the possibility the sheriff might have planted someone in nearby cells to eavesdrop.

"Why, that's—that's both wonderful and terrible," she whispered. "It means your father is dead, of course. He was such a fine man. But it, at least, proves that he was innocent of the terrible things they've said about him."

"The things Amos said, you mean," he said.

"Yes," she nodded. "Uncle Amos was the one. He's to blame. But why didn't you tell this to Mr. Benton? Or to Sheriff Rawls?"

"Clum knew I suspected Latzo," Steve said. "So he came to me and told me this, and asked me to lay off for fear I might drive Latzo deep into cover. Clum hoped that by watching Latzo he would eventually be able to round up the whole outfit in the train robberies and recover the money. If that money could be got back it'd save people in this basin plenty of grief."

"But——" she began. Then she fell silent.

"I know what you started to say," he said. "It's about Doug —and whether he's mixed up with Latzo. I believe the answer is no."

"But you're not sure?"

"I've got Doug's word for it. He never lied to me in the past. I know him well enough to feel that he's not lying now."

"He knows that you and I saw him that night?"

Steve nodded. "We're not very good at concealing things, I reckon. He guessed it from our attitudes. He came right out with it the other night after Amos and his Vigilantes had searched my place. That's why he pulled out. He was ashamed to face you, I suppose. I asked him whether he

116

was tied up with Latzo. He was insulted. He looked like he wanted to slug me. He despises Latzo."

"Then who is he tied up with?"

"He didn't say," Steve said. "I didn't ask. But, if there's any connection between his outfit and Latzo, he doesn't know about it. I'm as sure about that as you can be about any human being."

She drew a long breath. "I'm frightened. Terribly! I talked to Burl Talley. I met him outside the jail. He wasn't at all reassuring. He didn't want to come right out and say so, but he thinks you are guilty. And so does the town. And the town is quiet. Too quiet. The way people avoided me gave me the shivers."

Her slim hands were ice cold in his grasp. He could feel them trembling. He kissed her through the bars. "If it's lynching you're worrying about, forget it," he said, forcing himself to laugh at her fears. "Rawls won't stand for anything like that. He's a sincere officer, at least. But, even better, there must be other express company agents in town. Or will be soon, to take over where Clum left off. I'll straighten out everything as soon as I can talk to them."

She brightened. "I'll find them. But——"

"I don't dare confide in Rawls or Mart Lowery," he said. "They might give it away, or make a wrong move, and Latzo would be warned. He'd cover up good and tight and they'd never be able to prove anything."

"I—I hope you're right," she said. "But—but, if it's necessary, there's another way. All of this goes back to that moment when you hit Amos Whipple's gun arm. If it comes to that I'll tell them exactly why you did it."

"You won't have to," Steve said confidently. "Doug will do that himself."

"But, if he's left the Powderhorn——?"

"He'd come back when he found out that I was in a tight fix. And then too, I only think he may have pulled out. I don't know for certain."

"Are you sure he'd come back to help you?"

"Yes," Steve said.

"But he's weak. You know that also. Only a weak man would let himself become involved in the things he's mixed up in."

"Weak in some ways," Steve admitted. "And very headstrong and wild. Strong in others. Doug is a man who isn't

117

afraid to die. He proved that to me a long time ago. He told me how he got started in these robberies. He thinks he's responsible for killing an express messenger. They hold it over his head as a club to keep him with the gang."

"That sounds like an excuse," she said. "A club is a club only as long as you fear it."

She kissed him again. Her lips were soft and very yielding. "If—if anything happened to you . . ." she said shakily. She drew away.

"Where are you going?" he asked.

"To try to find these express men," she said as she hurried out of the jail room.

Chapter
Thirteen

Steve was taken into court that afternoon, handcuffed between Bill Rawls and Deputy Ed Walters. Carter Benton represented him at the arraignment, which was a brief, routine matter. Steve entered a plea of not guilty and waived a hearing. The judge bound him over to trial before the circuit court on a charge of murder.

The small courtroom, which adjoined the jail, was jammed with onlookers. What Eileen had told him was true. Bleak silence was the keynote of Bugle on this day. There was not a voice raised among the spectators, scarcely a murmur.

As Steve was led away that mood continued to hold. After he was back in his cell he could hear them leaving the courtroom and shuffling away along the sidewalk without talking.

Eileen returned late in the afternoon. This time Bill Rawls stood uncompromisingly at her elbow, listening to every word that was said.

"I—I couldn't find the men you mentioned, Steve," she said, worried. "They've either not arrived in Bugle yet, or are still out hunting the train robbers. The express office is closed and barred. Pete Crain can't be located. He's probably hiding somewhere, afraid of being mobbed because the company can't pay off."

Steve pondered it. Crain, as manager of Northern Express, was the one person likely to know the identity of any express operatives who might have been helping Clum.

"There won't be no mobbin' of nobody as long as I'm sheriff," Bill Rawls stated.

"How about Burl Talley?" Steve questioned Eileen. "Maybe Clum might have told him if there were other express agents handy."

"I asked Burl," she said. "He said Clum had never mentioned any. Apparently Clum was working alone."

She was trying to hide the deep concern that weighed on her. She kissed him and said, "I'll be back bright and early in the morning. I'll keep hunting them until I find them. Is there anything I can bring you?"

Steve looked at Rawls. "Yes," he said. "A sharp hacksaw, a six-shooter, and a fast horse."

Rawls smiled tolerantly. It was a jest he had heard many times. "Nobody's goin' to get out of this jail," he said. "An' nobody is gettin' in either without permission, if that's what's worrying you."

"That could be one of the things on my mind," Steve agreed.

"And mine," Eileen said.

Darkness came and Steve ate his evening meal. He smoked the last of the tobacco and paid the night turnkey to bring him a fresh supply. He kept rolling new smokes, lighting them, then crushing them out. He knew he was losing the battle to retain a semblance of sanity and calm.

The hush that had settled over the town during the day seemed to have hardened into something so tangible that he had the eerie sensation of its having taken the substance of a smothering blanket.

Sounds which would have been commonplace at another time had the jangling effect of breaking glass as they cut through this barrier. The indistinct voices of jailers and deputies in the office conducting routine duties appeared muted as though in tune with this mood.

This shield was torn violently aside. Gunfire broke out somewhere in the town. The heavy, slamming reports of .45's being fired with speed rolled through the night, the echoes recoiling from frame walls and false fronts.

Voices barked orders in the main office. Steve recognized one as belonging to Bill Rawls. Another's was Mart Lowery's. That faded away with a rush of men running from the office and down the street. The officers were hurrying to the scene of the disturbance.

The gunfire broke off. Steve decided that it had come from the gay district on Front Street. He could hear citizens in the street shouting questions at each other.

Then many riders swept into Bozeman Street and pulled up before the jail. The fast tread of boots sounded in the office. Hoarse, harsh orders were given and Steve heard the turnkey protesting halfheartedly.

The bolts were pulled on the inner door and men came flooding into the jail room. They had neckerchiefs tied over their faces and were prodding the turnkey ahead of them.

"Open that cell!" the leader commanded.

That was Amos Whipple's heavy voice. He had made no attempt to disguise it. Nor was the turnkey making any genuine effort to oppose them. The man shrugged and quickly unlocked the door of Steve's cell.

"Come out, Santee," Amos Whipple said.

Steve found himself facing leveled .45's. Hands seized him and tried to yank him through the door. He wrested free, slapped one pistol aside, and backed into the far corner of the cell.

"Come on, stranglers," he said bitterly. "Let's fight it out here."

He believed they would strike him down with bullets. He would welcome that rather than the lynching they evidently intended.

"Don't shoot him!" Amos Whipple shouted. "He's to get a fair chance to talk. A fair and square trial. Drag him out of there."

They rushed him. He fought grimly, swinging fists and boots at the mass of them. But he was overwhelmed by weight of numbers. His arms and legs were pinned down.

One of them drove a fist into his face and said, "You dirty killer. You'll have to talk fast."

Steve surged forward and rammed his head into the masked face and heard a grunt of pain. The man drew back a fist to batter Steve, but a tall member of the Vigilantes seized him by the shoulder and hurled him violently aside. "Yella blood!" the intruder raged. "Hitting a man who can't fight back."

"No brutality!" Amos Whipple boomed. "Keep your heads

men. We're not avengers. We are here only to see that justice is done."

Steve fought them futilely, but was dragged from the cell and through the office into the street. Horses were waiting along with other disguised, mounted men. The shooting on Front Street had been a ruse to draw Bill Rawls and the town marshal and their deputies away from the jail.

Bozeman Street was deserted. Appearance of the Vigilantes had driven all citizens discreetly to cover. Doors were closed and window curtains had heen tightly drawn.

But from Front Street the tinn: refrain of pianos and hurdy gurdies was rising again. Steve heard the hoarse monotone of a dancehall barker. Business was resuming as usual after the interruption of the gunfire. The word of what was happening at the jail had not yet spread that far.

Steve's wrists were lashed together. They lifted him into a saddle and one captor looped his ankles together with a thong beneath the horse.

The tall man who had saved him from being slugged in the cell began fumbling at the task of tying his bound hands to the saddlehorn.

Instead, Steve felt the metallic coolness of a knife blade against his wrists. The bonds loosened. They had been cut. The knife was left there between his locked hands, hidden.

Strong fingers closed reassuringly on his arm for an instant. Realization came! The tall Vigilante was Doug!

"All right!" Amos Whipple said, mounting and seizing up the trailing reins of Steve's horse.

The Vigilantes swung into the saddles and Amos led the way. The Pioneer House was a block west of the jail and Steve saw a feminine figure come from its door.

It was Eileen. She screamed something and raced toward the dark mass of riders, holding her skirts clear of the mud.

"Damn that girl!" Amos Whipple said.

Eileen was too far away, too late to intercept them. Amos led the way around the corner of the jail into a side street and pushed the pace to a gallop, leaving her still running futilely there in the street alone and screaming frenziedly for them to stop. The roar of hooves drowned out that outcry.

Steve realized that Doug was riding at his stirrup. They were passing through straggling back areas of town, heading northward. They entered a dark area of wagon yards and stock corrals and cattle pens and loading chutes which flanked the railroad yards.

Doug said, "Now!"

And he brought a rope slashing down on Steve's horse and his own. Steve saw the opening. It was a narrow lane between corrals, barely wide enough for a mounted man.

He tore his wrists free of the lashings and his horse made its first lunging stride. Wild shouts arose.

"Hey! Stop him! He's tryin'——! Shoot him! Shoot him! He's tryin' to make a break fer it!"

Steve's horse sped into the narrow lane at full gallop with Doug riding a length behind him.

"Hold your fire!" someone shouted. "That's one of our own boys chasin' him, right at his heels. You'll hit him instead o' Santee. He can't git away."

The Vigilantes were spurring in pursuit, but the lane was a bottleneck and their own numbers impeded them. Horses milled and reared in the darkness at the entrance.

Steve and Doug emerged into the open. They veered among shacks and ash heaps and crossed a series of sidetracks where empty cattle cars stood idle. They changed direction again, crossing the main line of the railroad and reached the rolling sagebrush flats northeast of town.

They pulled up to gain their bearings, and listened to the shouting and the distant mutter of hooves. Steve slashed the thong from his ankles. "Here's your knife, Doug," he said. "It came in handy."

He added, "I thought maybe you'd taken my advice and had pulled out of the Powderhorn."

They rode ahead again. Tumbleweeds formed grotesque shapes against the skyline as they mounted a low ridge. The search seemed to be swinging westward away from them.

The lights of Bugle began to fade behind. They passed over the rim of the rise and let the horses settle to a jiggling pace. They had shaken off the Vigilantes, whose big handicap had been their own numbers.

They traveled in silence for a time. Doug removed the neckerchief mask and hurled it away. "I know what you're thinking," he said. "I don't blame you. I let you take the jolt just to protect me. The real reason they believe you killed Frank Clum is because Amos has convinced them that you're in cahoots with the bunch who robbed the train. You expected to be strung up without me turning a hand to help you."

"I'll never come closer to going down the big chute," Steve admitted. "Amos talked about a fair trial. What he meant was a trial with a rope around my neck."

"I'd have talked before it went that far," Doug said, his voice dull. "I was in a saloon on Front Street last night when I heard that you had been arrested for Clum's murder. I knew what the next move would be, for I know my father. So I high-tailed it out to Center Fire."

"Center Fire?"

"I siwashed out in the brush not far from the house last night, keeping an eye on the place," Doug said. "I knew any move that would be made by the Vigilantes would start from there. I was there when Burl Talley brought the news of Clum's murder to Amos this morning."

"Talley?" Steve repeated. "Was he with the Vigilantes?"

"I doubt if he was in the bunch that came to the jail," Doug said. "Burl never was one to get mixed up in real trouble. But he helped notify other ranchers in the organization. I kept cases on Amos, knowing he was the leader. They all met at the Spanish Flat schoolhouse after dark. I eavesdropped and heard them arrange that fake gunfight to decoy the law away from the jail. I pulled on a mask and joined the party, mixing in with them in the dark as they rode up to the jail. They never knew they had an extra member."

"You must have been watching them when they set fire to my house," Steve said. "What else did they do there?"

"Set fire to your house?" Doug exclaimed. "That's the first I've heard of that. Do you mean that? When did that happen?"

"Last night sometime, evidently," Steve said.

"Amos couldn't have had anything to do with it," Doug said. "At least he was at Center Fire all night, asleep in his bed, to the best of my knowledge. You mean your house is gone—burned down?"

"So Bill Rawls told me," Steve said.

Doug waited, but he added nothing more to that. Doug misunderstood his silence. "I know what you're wondering," he said. "You're thinking that maybe I'm mixed up in Clum's murder."

Steve twisted in the saddle, gazing at him in the darkness. "Now that you've brought it up," he said. "Maybe I am."

"I had nothing to do with it, actually," Doug said dully. "But maybe I'm mixed up in it by what the law would call guilt by association."

"Who killed Clum?" Steve demanded.

"I don't know that."

"Maybe you know someone who does know?"

"I'm not even sure about that," Doug said. "I could be wrong. Dead wrong."

"You mean you don't want to tell me because of outlaw honor? You won't turn against your pals even though they killed a man in cold blood. Is that it?"

"It wasn't the ones who were in on the train robbery with me," Doug said miserably. "I'm sure of that, at least. They were playing poker in the same Front Street gambling house I was in when Clum was murdered. They had been there all evening. None of them could have done it."

"You don't want to tell me who those men are?"

"No," Doug said. "I guess you named it. Outlaw honor. I can't be an informer, Steve."

"A man tried to kill me last night at my house," Steve said. "Someone must have sent him to do the job. I was lucky. He missed. Before it was over I got him. Something I found in his pocket warned me that Clum might be in for the same treatment. That's why I rode to town. I was just a few minutes too late to save him."

"Who was it who tried to get you?" Doug asked.

"I never saw him before. Hard-cased type with big crooked teeth, nose flattened at the bridge, coarse black hair. Might have a touch of Indian or Spanish blood. Wore——"

"Choctaw!" Doug exclaimed.

"Who's Choctaw?"

"One of Nick Latzo's flunkies. At least the description fits him. Hung around the Silver Moon. Worked as case keeper for faro dealers at times. Bad medicine. The kind that'd cut a throat for a price. But Bill Rawls could have told you who he was if it was really Choctaw. Didn't Rawls——?"

"Trouble is Rawls said his deputy couldn't find any sign of a dead man in the saddle shed, where I had carried the body," Steve said. "It wasn't until this morning that he sent Ed Walters out there to take a look. Someone must have got there first and moved Choctaw elsewhere. There wasn't even a bloodstain, according to Walters. That's when he found that the house had been burned. It must have been the same person—or persons."

As he spoke Steve again shifted the direction in which they traveled. They had been heading north toward the river. Now he swung eastward, paralleling the course of the stream in its widening loop through the basin.

"We'll be hitting the main road to the ford any minute," Doug warned. "Somebody might sight us. Where are you going?"

"To the Silver Moon," Steve said.

Doug drew a harsh, startled breath. "Jupiter, but you do pick 'em tough!" he said almost joyously. He touched his horse with a spur, an eagerness and a wildness rising in him as he moved up to ride side by side.

Chapter
Fourteen

They left the horses hidden in the brush and moved in on the Silver Moon, halting on the fringe of the clearing. The hour, Steve judged, was nearing nine o'clock and business at the roadhouse was at its evening peak.

A score of saddle animals were tethered at the rails, along with buggies and buckboards which had brought patrons from the mining camps in the hills. The orchestra, which had been playing for dancers, now struck a crashing chord, then quieted.

A man's voice made an announcement. Cowboy yells arose and the music struck up again. A woman began singing.

The way was clear and they moved swiftly to the side of the building, huddling in shadow. Through a slit in a curtained window Steve saw an entertainer on the small stage. It was Daisy O'Day.

Some of the gambling had slowed while players turned their attention to the stage, but other games were progressing without interruption.

Nick Latzo was not present. Steve surmised that he was at

the Blue Moon in town as usual. But Louie Latzo stood at the rear corner of the bar, a drink in his hand. Louie was smoking a cigar and wore a silk vest and a pleated linen shirt with a pearl stickpin in the flowery cravat. A gray derby hat was perched on his head.

Daisy O'Day finished her song and returned for an encore in response to loud applause which was led by Louie himself. Steve kept his attention on Louie. Doug nudged him and pointed. Al Painter sat in the lookout high seat. In another part of the room Chick Varney mingled with patrons. Both men were on duty as trouble shooters, for they each packed braces of six-shooters. They bore the court plaster and livid marks of their combat with Steve and Doug.

The singing ended. Louie hastened to offer his arm to Daisy O'Day and they walked through the door that led to the areas back stage.

This was the chance for which Steve had been hoping. He moved along the outside wall, ducking below the line of the windows. Doug followed.

Steve had visited the Silver Moon in the past, and while he was not familiar with the interior in this part of the structure, he remembered that there had been an outer stage entrance at the far corner.

He reached this door and found it open. Louie and Daisy O'Day were approaching along the inner passageway. Steve and Doug crouched down and heard a key creak in a lock.

Steve chanced a look. The pair were entering a varnished door which he was sure admitted them to Nick Latzo's living quarters.

The girl, who had drawn a wrap around her, preceded Louie through the portal. There was no one else in the passageway.

"Stay out of this," he told Doug. "Don't let anyone see you."

He leaped forward, covering the dozen feet in two strides and drove his shoulder against the startled Louie, propelling him violently ahead into the center of the room where he went staggering to his hands and knees.

Steve pounced on him and locked his fingers around the man's throat. "Steady," he said. "Or I'll break your neck, Louie."

Doug, ignoring the warning, entered a pace behind him and closed the door.

Daisy O'Day had stood frozen. "What the hell . . . !" she began. Her voice squeaked off. Steve was not armed, but Doug wore a six-shooter. He had not drawn the gun, but it wasn't necessary. The entertainer knew that big trouble had arrived.

"Just stay quiet and keep out of this, lady," Steve said. "You're not in this."

He snatched Louie to his feet, searched him, and removed a short-muzzled pistol from an armpit holster and a derringer from a sleeve. Also a wicked dirk from a belt scabbard. "Do you like knives, Louie?" he asked.

He pushed Louie against a wall and held him pinned there, his fingers wrapped in the front of the fancy vest. "Don't make a sound," he said.

He turned Louie's pockets out, spilling the contents on the floor. Finally a billfold emerged, and this he kicked toward Doug. "See what's in it," he said.

It contained several bills but none were in the hundred-dollar denomination that Steve had hoped might be there. But he had hardly counted on Louie being careless enough to have kept such evidence on him.

"You've spent it already, I suppose," he said. "It was you, all right, that I sighted spooking out of the Pioneer House as Clum was dying with a knife in his back in his room. You killed him, Louie, and spent some of that two hundred dollars on this fine plumage you're wearing. And you likely know who murdered my father. It was your brother, Nick, wasn't it?"

Louie was ash-pale. His eyes were blank and distended with fear. He expected to be shot with his own gun, which Steve jammed into his stomach.

"What happened to Choctaw's body?" Steve demanded.

"I don't know what you're talkin' about!" Louie gasped.

"You're lying," Steve said. "I'd kill you myself, Louie, but you're going to swing for the murder of Frank Clum and Buck Santee. And Nick too. I make that promise to you."

He shoved Louie toward the door. "You're going with me," he said. "We'll see if you can't be persuaded to remember a few things that I want to know."

Then he and Doug stood listening to the sound of footsteps in the passageway. A hand tapped on the door. "Louie!" a voice called. "Is it all right if Dude Lacey takes over the deal at the number two table? Whitey's gone into another of his coughin' spells."

That was the voice of Al Painter.

"Say yes," Steve whispered.

Louie tried. He tried again. A third time. But no sound issued from his fear-frozen lips.

Painter pounded the door harder and impatiently. "Louie! Do you hear me?"

Daisy O'Day gathered her courage and screamed wildly. "Two gunmen have got Louie!" she screeched. "They're sluggin' him around and are goin' to take him with them."

Her voice carried through the thin-walled building. It evidently reached the main room for Steve heard the music and the shuffle of dancing feet halt abruptly.

He spoke to Doug. "Come on! We're going out!"

He opened the door and pushed Louie ahead of him into the passageway, clinging to the wilting collar of the man's shirt with one hand, the gun in his other grip.

Al Painter had backed away a few paces and had drawn his brace of pistols. But he could not fire without killing Louie. Beyond them Steve saw Chick Varney come rushing into the passageway, a pair of guns also in his hands.

"Don't shoot, Al!" Louie babbled.

Steve and Doug backed through the outer door by which they had entered. Steve knew it was impossible now to take Louie with them.

Once they were in the open starlight he sent Louie spinning to the ground with a shove. He and Doug raced for the brush. But, even as they turned, a gun exploded almost at their feet.

It was Louie who had fired. He had snatched from some hide-out in his coat a double-barreled derringer that Steve had missed while searching him.

He had aimed at the back of Doug, who was nearest him. He was now twisting around as he lay on the ground to bring the second barrel of the little, vicious gun into play against Steve at that short range.

Steve flipped back the hammer of the pistol he had seized from the man and fired. The bullet must have torn through Louie's arm or shoulder, for the derringer flew from his hand

and exploded as it hit the ground. Louie's body was jerked around and he uttered a moaning sound.

Steve and Doug raced for the trees. "Are you all right, Doug?" Steve asked.

"Yes," Doug said.

Six-shooters opened up on them from the roadhouse. Al Painter was trying to bring them down as he crouched in the doorway through which they had emerged. At another point Chick Varney sent window glass shattering as he cleared an opening through which to shoot. His guns joined in the uproar.

A bullet ripped bark from an alder, the fragments showering Steve's face. Another glanced from a tree trunk, buzzing between him and Doug.

They reached deeper shelter in the thickets and changed direction. Slugs raked the brush in an attempt to bring them down. Painter and Varney were shooting blind now, and that failed. The guns went empty.

They located their horses, hit the saddles, and rode away, heading southward. The shouting around the roadhouse receded and was lost as they built up distance. Evidently the patrons of the Silver Moon did not deem it worth while to join in a fight the origin of which was not clear to them, and Varney and Painter lacked the courage, for there was no pursuit.

After a mile or two they left the brush and circled Bugle to the south, swinging gradually westward toward the upper basin and the mountains. The lights of the town were bright and steady only two miles to their right.

They crossed Long Ridge and entered the clearing in which stood the Spanish Flat schoolhouse. It was dark and silent in the moonlight. The main trail from town curved past within a few rods of the structure, and they pulled up to listen. There was no sound.

"Where to?" Doug asked. It was the first word either of them had spoken.

"I wish I knew," Steve said. "You shouldn't have shown your face in that roadhouse, Doug. They'll shoot you on sight now, the same as they will me. Up to that time I doubt if anyone knew you were the man who helped me get away from the Vigilantes. Rawls will probably know it soon."

"It was time I showed my face on one side or the other, wasn't it?" Doug said. There was a thickening quality in his tone that Steve took for anger and weariness.

"You were wrong about one thing, Doug," he said. "Nick Latzo is mixed up in the train holdups. And Louie too, most likely. You know that now, don't you?"

"Yes," Doug said in blurred tone. "But I didn't know it until I saw that look in Louie's eyes. You were right. He's the one who knifed Clum."

"Somebody with a lot of savvy has been maneuvering these holdups," Steve said. "He directed suspicion at Nick Latzo so as to keep the law running in circles on a wild goose chase. He fooled Frank Clum and he fooled Bill Rawls. Clum was so certain that Latzo was his man that he played right into the hands of the person he least suspected. Latzo was a party to the scheme. But he was only a decoy."

"He was more than a decoy when he sent men to kill you and Clum," Doug said.

"Somebody must have told Latzo that Clum had evidence which might hang him for the murder of my father," Steve said. "That's my guess. And that someone also feared Clum would eventually learn too much about the train robberies. That same person probably guessed that I had recognized you as one of the long riders. So, for his own safety, he decided that both Clum and I must be put out of the way. Nick Latzo had the means of that kind of an operation. He has men at his call who'll kill for a price. So this man turned the job over to him."

He quit talking for a while. "And now, do you want to tell me the name of that man?" he finally asked.

"You probably won't believe this, but up to this moment I was no more sure of who he is than you were," Doug said.

"What?"

"I suspected it," Doug said. "But it seemed so fantastic I couldn't convince myself. The only ones I was sure about were the men I went with on the two holdups. I never saw the one who planned the jobs. But I know now who it is. And I can see that you know also."

"Clum told me that he believed none of the money from the three holdups has appeared in circulation," Steve said. "He thought that all of it was still intact somewhere—hidden in or near the basin."

"That's the way it's supposed to be," Doug nodded. "The

agreement was that the money is to be kept in one chunk until we have enough to keep us well off for the rest of our lives. Then it'll be divided and we split up. Some of us talked of going to South America. It was up to one man to decide when we had enough. I was to get my cut from the last two holdups. I wasn't in on the first one."

"You mean you don't know where the money is hidden?" Steve asked. "Clum said it amounts to close to a quarter of a million dollars, including the Pool fund."

"I don't know where it's cached," Doug admitted. "I've been played for a sucker both ways from the middle. I realize that. But I didn't have much choice after that express messenger was killed. I've done a lot of drinking lately, Steve. An awful lot. I can't think straight anymore. I know that—that—you—and—Eileen——"

His words dwindled off. In the starlight Steve saw him sag suddenly in the saddle. Before he could prevent it Doug slipped to the ground with the flabbiness of an empty sack. His spur hung in a stirrup. His horse began to rear, but Steve leaped to the ground and freed his boot.

Steve fumbled for a match and finally got one lighted. Doug lay crumpled on his side, his face the color of a wax candle. One side of his coat was soggy and sticky with blood.

The derringer slug that Louie Latzo had fired had found its target, but Doug, rather than chance any slowing of Steve's escape, had refused to admit that he had been wounded.

The bullet had torn upward, burning a gouge along his ribs, and had buried itself in the heavy muscles below the shoulder blade. Steve could feel the hard pellet just under the skin.

He ignited another match and another, ignoring the danger that this might reveal him to manhunters. He decided that the injury itself was not the kind that would be fatal to a man of Doug's endurance. But the loss of blood was another matter.

He became aware that a rider was approaching at a fast lope up the trail from the direction of town. He lifted Doug and carried him to the schoolhouse.

The frame-built structure, like its kind, was determinedly oblong with a shingled gable roof which supported a small bell tower. A wooden awning guarded the main door at the front, but there was a rear door which opened abruptly into a bare clearing which served as a play yard. The front door bore a padlock but Steve had better luck at the rear entrance. It was latched, but the hasp was loose and the screws that held it came free almost at the touch of his hand.

He carried Doug inside and laid him on the floor in darkness. He raced back and led the horses to the far side of the building out of sight of the trail.

The lone rider came abreast of the school property at that same high pace. The horse Steve had been riding scented the other animals and blew suddenly and loudly.

The rider drew up instantly, then swung around and came directly toward the schoolhouse. Steve drew his six-shooter. He peered at the silhouette of the arrival against the stars.

"Eileen!" he exclaimed.

She dismounted and rushed to him. "I knew it must be you when I heard the horse," she said. "I was on my way to Antler, thinking you might try to get in touch with me there. Steve! Steve! Are you all right?"

"I am," he said. "But Doug's here. Wounded. My fault. I went to the Silver Moon to try to make Louie Latzo talk. It ended in a gun fight."

He led her inside the building and chanced igniting a match. He found a quantity of loose paper and lighted spills. They cut away Doug's jacket and used his shirt for bandages.

The bleeding stopped. Steve brought water in his hat from the creek. That strengthened Doug and he mumbled, "Eileen, get out of here. Stay away from me. I'm poison! Bad!"

He tried to rise to his feet. He did not make it. Steve caught him as he fell and lifted him, supporting him.

"Somebody's bound to search this schoolhouse before the night's over," he said. "Do you think you can hang on for a few miles in the saddle, Doug?"

"Ten miles," Doug mumbled gamely. "Twenty. You name it."

Eileen led up the horses and Steve carried Doug into the open and boosted him into the saddle. Doug reeled, but hung on. Steve and Eileen mounted and moved in at his side and steadied him.

"Where are we going?" Doug asked.

"To a place where you'll be safe," Steve said. "And cared for."

He looked at Eileen and she understood and nodded.

They moved away from Spanish Flat at a slow pace. For some time Doug was too weak and spent to think or ask questions.

Suddenly he aroused, gazing at the mountain skyline against the Milky Way. They were fording a small, shallow creek. "Little Canteen Creek!" he said. "We're near Center Fire—near home!"

They emerged from timber and the scattered buildings and corrals of Amos Whipple's sizeable headquarters lay before them beneath the midnight sky. No light showed.

"Your mother will be there," Steve said.

Doug said violently, "No! I won't——!"

"You've got to have help—and love," Eileen told him.

She dismounted and ran across the clearing to the house, making no sound that might arouse the two or three riders who, no doubt, were sleeping in the bunkhouse.

Presently she returned and said, "All right."

Steve lifted Doug, still mumbling protests, from the saddle and half carried him to the house. The kitchen door was open, but no lamp had been lighted.

Julia Whipple, a kindly, careworn pioneer woman, took her straying son in her arms and wept over him for a moment.

The house was a two-story frame structure. Julia Whipple led the way with a shaded lamp and Steve carried Doug up the stairs and placed him on a bed.

There, with blinds drawn, he stripped off Doug's clothes and left the remainder of the task to his mother and Eileen.

It was more than an hour before Eileen finally joined him in the dimly-lit kitchen where he was drinking coffee and eating cold beef and bread which he had found in the pantry.

"We've done all we can do here," she said. "Aunt Julia can handle it now. He's much better. We've given him broth and the juice from canned tomatoes. That's what he needs most of all to replace lost blood. He'll probably come out of it in a hurry."

"What did you tell her?" he asked.

"Only that he was shot helping a friend and that it would be better if no one was to know where he is."

"But how can she prevent Amos from knowing?" he asked.

"Aunt Julia says Amos has never set foot in Doug's room since Doug left Center Fire. The door has been kept closed and locked. I'm sure Doug will need to be there only a day or two."

Steve debated it and decided it was the safest place for the wildling. Now that he had a chance to think it over he doubted that the Latzos would want to talk to Bill Rawls about what had happened at the roadhouse, for that might lead to some questions about the reason for Steve's visit there that might be awkward to answer. Only Louie and the two gunmen knew that Doug was the man who had accompanied him. They likely would prefer to settle the matter themselves, but they hardly would risk coming to Center Fire, even if they suspected Doug was there.

"All right," he said, and arose.

He concealed Doug's saddle in the wagon shed and told Julia Whipple where it could be found. He and Eileen rode away, leading Doug's horse. They turned it loose on open range a few miles away.

He reached out, laid his hand on Eileen's on the saddle-horn. "It's been a long night," he said. "You'll be home and in your bed in thirty minutes. Will you be afraid to make it alone? You'll be safe enough, even if it's three in the morning and dark as the inside of a whale."

"I'm not afraid of the dark. I never was. But where are you going?"

"First I want to take a look-see at my saddle shed where I left Choctaw's body."

"Choctaw?"

"Doug thinks that's the name of the man I told Bill Rawls about. The one who tried to kill me. Maybe I want to convince myself I didn't dream about that fight. Maybe I want to prove something. Next, come daybreak, I want to be up on Cardinal Mountain, watching at a wolf hole."

"I just love to watch wolf holes," she said.

"You're going home."

"There are no wolf dens at Antler. At least none worth wasting time watching. And I couldn't stand it—the waiting. It's all settled. You can't leave me behind."

"You might be shaped up considerably better," Steve said. "But you're still the same bullheaded imp who made a pest of herself to Doug and me when we were kids."

"Thank you for complimenting me on my shape at least," she said. "Do you really think it has improved?"

"Indeed I do," Steve said. "But the question under discussion was about you going home peacefully."

"I'm not going home peacefully or otherwise," she said. "That's all been decided. And don't try to force me to go. I can kick and scratch."

"How well I remember," Steve sighed.

Chapter
Fifteen

They rode toward Steve's ranch. Avoiding the trail as much as possible, they kept to the shadow of brush and timber.

As they neared Canteen Creek the odor of wet, charred wood rode the night—a dismal presence as of the smell of death.

They came out into the open meadow beneath the stars and Steve watched the ears of their mounts, feeling that the animals would be the first to warn them if there were humans or other horses around. But they gave no sign of uneasiness. His ranch was unguarded as yet.

He led the way nearer. The ruins of the house bulked up in a deformed pattern. There seemed to be little chance that anything could be salvaged. Only portions of the half-burned log walls still stood. Steve's father had cut and shaped those logs with his own ax and adz.

Steve dismounted and entered the saddle shed. He ignited one of his dwindling supply of matches. The lamp he had placed on the bench still stood where he had left it. He lighted it.

The feedbox on which he had laid the body was a six-foot-long container, built of sheet metal nailed to a wooden frame and divided into two compartments for the storage of corn and bran. The last fragments of the grain had long ago been cleaned out by packrats and mice.

The cover of the box had been built stoutly of the pine siding of a packing case. It was missing. Steve was certain that the porous, unpainted pine would have carried bloodstains. But the lid had been carried away.

135

Eileen watched him from the doorway as he peered around. The dust of disuse had accumulated in the shed, but many boots and many hands had disturbed this layer on the floor and benches until there was little hope that anything could be learned from this source. Evidently Deputy Ed Walters had gone over the place and no doubt there had been other curiosity-minded visitors.

"Someone—or maybe more than one—got here long before Rawls sent his deputy to take a look-see," he said. "They probably buried Choctaw's body somewhere. It had been raining and it would have been easy to have caved in a cutbank over the grave, or a sandy bluff. The place might not be far away, or it could be miles off. Whether it will ever be found is anybody's guess. Trying to hunt it would be like looking for a lost needle. We might as well ride. There's nothing here to help us."

They mounted again and he led the way across country to the Powderhorn. They forded the stream with the morning star beginning to burn with diamond-white brilliance in the sky. The cold river rushed around the legs of the horses, sighing a sad song.

Eileen pulled her horse closer, reached out, and Steve felt her fingers creep into his hand and hold tightly. "I'm always afraid of rivers at night," she said. "They frighten me. They are so strange."

The horses waded ashore and left the sighing behind. Dawn was at hand. The Milky Way began to fade. The mountains took somber form, rearing up as a black wall against the sky. Soon the peaks stood defined in pastel gray. A lilac hue formed at the crests and the snowfields caught the first rosy tint of the coming sun. Around them this wild, tumbled world emerged, ridge upon ridge, deep shadow upon shadow. Daybreak!

New shell ice tinkled beneath the hooves of the horses in the shallows along the small streams. Steve felt the cold bite through his jacket. The sun edged above the horizon as they climbed higher on the mountain. Its warmth, feeble at first, touched their cheeks.

Steve became cautious as they neared the location of the hide-out to which Eileen had led him the day of the elk hunt. He circled the area, scanning the ground for tracks.

He became satisfied the place was deserted. He rode to a rise which commanded a wide view of the river and the basin. The smoke of morning cookfires in Bugle rose above Long Ridge. "All right," he said and lifted Eileen to the ground. "I'm going to search that dugout. You stand lookout. If you see anyone, whistle a couple of times. Stay off the skylines."

"The money?" she questioned.

"Yes. I doubt if it's here. But it might be. I've got to make sure. Up to now I can't offer one shred of actual evidence against anyone. Nothing but suspicion, and conclusions at which I've arrived by fitting together a lot of happenings that didn't seem to make sense at first. There's only one solid proof that would be enough to convince a man like Amos Whipple. Or Bill Rawls. Possession of the stolen money itself."

"And who do you suspect?" she asked.

"Maybe you've already guessed," he said.

"I—I don't know," she said uncertainly. "The things I think frighten me."

He left her and walked on foot down the game trail to the hidden dugout, his footprints plain in the thin coating of frost which rimmed the grass. There he went over the interior foot by foot, probing and tapping in search of any cavity in which treasure might have been cached.

He roved the thickets in the vicinity. He took pains to avoid leaving any easily-seen evidence of his presence. The frost was evaporating with the warming of the air and his footprints disappeared along with it.

He was keeping at the search, determined to exhaust every possibility, when Eileen whistled a warning. He hurried back to the ridge where she waited, concealed among the rimrock.

"Two riders just forded the river and are heading up the mountain," she said. "They were too far off to make out who they are."

They waited. Presently Steve sighted the pair a long distance away and down the mountain. They were tiny, moving dots which vanished into timber.

After an interval, the two appeared in a wide grassy clearing along a stream in which a score or more of loose horses grazed. They cut five animals from the bunch and hazed them off into the trees, heading up the mountain in the direction of the hide-out.

Steve looked at Eileen, elated. "Maybe this trip up here

will pan out after all," he said. "Every smart wolf has more than one way out of his den. Maybe we came to the right place after all."

"Did you recognize them?" she asked. "Who are they?"

He looked at her. "Burl Talley expects to marry you, doesn't he?" he asked.

She became indignant. "I make my own decisions in matters like that," she said.

Steve laughed. "That's another question that hardly needed an answer. I should have known better than to ask."

"And just what was the answer?" she demanded.

"The right one," he said.

Leading the horses on foot, they retreated nearly half a mile from the hide-out and took deep cover among boulders and aspen. Steve found a cranny among the rocks. The sun reflected warmth upon them, and Eileen leaned against him, heavy-eyed from loss of sleep. He knew she was also hungry.

"We got separated from the chuckwagon somewhere along the way," he said. "You'll have to take a notch in your belt."

A quarter of an hour passed. Then he nudged her. They watched a rider appear in the open draw which led to the hide-out in the thicket.

It was Tex Creed. The man pulled up, gazing around, and circled the draw, but his attitude was that of one who felt that he was unobserved. Then he rode down the game trail into the thicket toward the hide-out.

"I've known it for some time," Eileen whispered. "At least I began to guess it yesterday. But I still couldn't believe it. It just couldn't be. It's—it's impossible."

He nodded. "Everything points to it. When we met Creed and Highriver the day of the elk hunt they weren't really riding posse. That was only an excuse for diverting other men away from this part of the mountain—and also to turn loose the horses that had been corraled there for emergency in case anything went wrong and they had to slope out of the country in a hurry."

"How long have you suspected all this?"

"About the same time you did, I suppose. I started piecing items together."

"What's Creed doing now?" she asked.

"Making sure someone isn't using the hide-out. Doug, for instance."

Creed reappeared and waved his hat in a signal. After a

short wait the five loose horses came streaming into the draw. They were being driven by the swarthy Highriver.

"Two pack animals," Steve said. "The rest are saddle stock."

Creed joined Highriver in pushing the horses out of sight down the game trail. The two men soon returned and rode off down the mountain in the direction of the river ford. They kept to cover as much as possible.

Steve studied them as long as they were in sight. They were riding high in the saddle, stiff-legged and straight-backed. They were pushing the horses. They had all the earmarks of men who were on edge and had some pressing purpose in mind.

"They're running scared," he told Eileen. "I've got a hunch our wolf is going to be forced out in the open where I can get a chance at him. And soon. Mighty soon."

She was gazing at him questioningly. "Too many things have happened that they don't like," he explained. "Clum's murder, for one. My escape from jail for another. And Doug's disappearance. They may have heard about Choctaw too. Things are happening that they probably don't understand. My guess is they're getting ready to light out to save their necks."

He caught up the horses and they rode to the dugout. The five animals were locked in the structure and munching grain. The two pack horses and one of the saddle mounts bore Amos Whipple's Center Fire brand. The other two belonged to Eileen's Antler string.

"Just look at that," Eileen said indignantly. "Our best cutting horses. That's Biscuit, and the roan is Old Sarge. Shorty Barnes would hit the ceiling if he knew outlaws were making free use of our top stock."

"If you were going to pick relay horses to get you over Cardinal Pass ahead of the sheriff you wouldn't pick crowbait," Steve commented.

He freed the animals and sent them scattering down the mountain. "That'll give them some trouble if they try to use this route out," he said.

"This wolf isn't likely to be stopped as easily as that," Eileen said shakily. Tension was growing in her. "And the proper way of referring to him is in the plural. This wolf is not one man alone. We've already seen two. And we're sure who the leader of the pack is."

"Are we?" he asked.

"It's time we started calling him by his right name," she said. "Burl Talley. He's back of all this."

Steve nodded. "He was the only one in a position to do a number of things that happened that couldn't all be put down to coincidence. In the first place Clum confided in him, believing him to be a man of integrity. That was a fatal error for Clum. It gave Talley the whip hand. He knew every move Clum made. And evidently he guessed that I had recognized Doug during the train holdup. He didn't want that information to go any farther. He decided we had to be put out of the way. He's the one who planted those hundred-dollar bills."

"What about Nick Latzo?" she asked. "Where does he figure in this?"

"I'm not sure, but my hunch is that they're secret partners. Even Doug didn't know that Talley was the brain back of the train robberies. Creed was the active leader. Talley never risked his own hide by taking part openly in the holdups. Creed and Highriver are reckless men, but they aren't cold-blooded killers. When it came to having murder done Talley had to go to Latzo, who had cutthroats in his crowd."

They rode lower on the mountain and halted at a vantage point. After more than an hour they watched Creed and Highriver recross the river.

The two men were now leading three spare horses which they had picked up from the stock grazing the benches. They headed up the basin in the direction of Bugle, but kept to the timber and broken country along the river.

"There's no way of telling for sure at this distance," Steve said, "but I'd be willing to bet that two of those horses are pack animals too. They're going to set another relay near town. Our wolf must still be in Bugle. At least that seems to be where the pack is congregating. I'd have thought that Talley's Rafter O would be a more likely hiding place."

"You think that holdup money might be right in town?"

"It's got to be somewhere close. It looks to me like they're staking out pack horses for insurance in case they have to ride far and fast. Most of the money taken in the three holdups was in gold, I understand. You can't just pack a hundred thousand dollars or so in gold around in your saddlebags. I figure that's about what the share for three men would amount to. For it looks like three of them are intending to pull out. My guess is that the other one is that mill boss, Whitey Bird. He seemed to be pretty thick with Creed and Highriver."

They left the mountain and also forded the Powderhorn. Eileen turned in the direction of Antler. "Food!" she said. "I'm famished and so are you. It's only a mile or two out of the way, and we can overtake them before they reach town if that's where they're going. I doubt if your wolf will make any kind of a move in broad daylight anyway. Wolves prefer to work in the dark."

She added, "Speaking of broad daylight, you haven't forgotten, I hope, that you are still being hunted. No doubt there's a reward on your head by this time. Burl Talley will see to that. You must be careful. There are some people who will be only too happy to shoot you on sight."

Steve thought of the easy ways of life he had visualized when he had stood on the station platform at Junction Bend only a few days in the past. He looked down at himself. He ran his hand over his unshaven jaws.

"You look like a pirate," Eileen said.

"Or a train robber," he said.

Nearing Antler ranch he waited at a distance while she rode in. She returned presently, bringing food and a .45 pistol and a holster and belt. "They belonged to Dad," she said.

She also brought a fresh saddle horse for him, a roan. And gray range hat and a blue flannel shirt to replace the black headgear and the ragged shirt he had been wearing.

"At least they'll have to take a second look at you before they begin shooting," she said. "These clothes belong to Shorty Barnes. He's at the ranch. He asked no questions and therefore I did not have to tell him any fibs. He looked at me more in sorrow than accusation. He thinks I'm a fallen woman. After all, I was away all night, you know."

"What else does he think?"

"That I'm helping a man wanted for murder. Al Painter and Chick Varney were snooping around the ranch early this morning, Shorty says. They claimed they'd been deputized to hunt you. Shorty says he's sure they were also trying to find out if I was home. Shorty told them I was still asleep. They were heading for your place when they pulled out. He figures they'll be back."

She watched him buckle on the holster. He thrust the short-muzzled six-shooter he had been carrying into a saddle pocket.

She moved close, put her arms around him and clung to him tightly. "Where's this going to end?" she asked huskily.

"In Bugle, I hope," he said gently. "And soon."

"I—I don't want to lose you now after waiting all my life for you," she said.

He kissed her, gravely at first and then with a wild rush. "There's no other way," he said. "They've got to be caught redhanded—if they're to be caught."

He added, "It would be best if you stayed here."

For once, she did not oppose him. He mounted then and rode away. He looked back before the run of the timber intervened. She had climbed into the saddle of her mount and was spurring away at a lope.

He rode up the basin, staying off the trails. He crowded the horse faster.

It was noon and the day was turning hot when he reached the crest of Long Ridge two miles from town. He sighted Creed and Highriver. They were just entering the outskirts of Bugle. They no longer had the three spare animals with them. Steve was certain he had estimated the situation correctly. The horses had been left in hiding not far from town.

The two men vanished among the buildings in the heart of the settlement. Steve dismounted, drew the rigging from the roan, rubbed it down with dry grass and hung the sweaty saddle blanket on a bush. He sat with his back against a fir tree, preparing his mind for patient vigil.

Chapter
Sixteen

Bugle lay peaceful in the sunlight. Ore wagons crawled down the trails from the mines at intervals and unloaded their cargoes down the chutes in the railroad yards, the sound drifting in lazy, booming echoes.

Riders and harness rigs arrived and departed. A lumber

dray, carrying fat lengths of freshly-fallen yellow pine and drawn by a jerkline hitch entered town, bound for Burl Talley's sawmill. A load of milled lumber, including window and door framing from the planing mill pulled out, bound for mining camps in the Powderhorns. Housewives hung clothes on lines in the yards of homes in the town.

The man in whom Steve was interested did not emerge. He began dozing off into short snatches of rest, disciplining his mind to bring him awake at intervals of a quarter of an hour or less, at which times he would sit up and scan any travelers on the roads. Then he would drift off again.

Thus passed the afternoon. The shadows of the mountains marched across the basin. Sundown's coolness touched him and he aroused completely.

He waited until twilight lay deep upon the town. Mounting, he rode nearer, measuring his pace so that he entered the outskirts under cover of full early darkness.

He followed a back street and finally tethered his horse in deep shadow just off Bozeman Street. He walked to the corner and peered.

Burl Talley's lumberyard fronted on Bozeman Street at this point. The office occupied a frame structure which abutted on the sidewalk at the corner farthest from the point where Steve stood. The lumberyard, where it faced the main thoroughfare, was guarded by a high board fence, pierced by a wagon gate with double wings. The gate was closed. The planing mill occupied a ramshackle structure at the rear of the property.

The door of the office was closed, but two swinging oil lamps burned in the room. A sash in one of the two windows overlooking the sidewalk was raised for air.

Only one person was visible in the office. Tex Creed. He sat in a swivel chair, smoking a cigarette. He flipped this away, but soon was nervously rolling another. He occupied the chair in the same taut, on-edge manner that Steve had marked in his posture on a horse earlier in the day.

A passer-by was approaching on the sidewalk. This compelled Steve to pull back into concealment until the man had gone by.

He returned to his viewpoint. Presently Creed went to the door and gazed down Bozeman Street with the fretful manner of a man waiting for someone who was wasting precious time.

Steve became aware of activity in the dark, closed lumberyard. He heard the occasional stamp of hooves and the clink of bit chains. He saw the flare of matches being applied to smokes. At least two men were waiting in the depths of the place, along with livestock.

Passers-by and riders and vehicles moved up and down Bozeman Street, driving him into cover each time. Bill Rawls came riding by, accompanied by Ed Walters and another deputy. They were soggy with weariness. Steve guessed they were returning from running down some blind trail. Rawls had not only the train robbery as his responsibility now but Steve's escape from jail also. No doubt persons with vivid imaginations were seeing fugitives back of every tree and bush and keeping the law busy on useless searching.

The sheriff turned off at the jail three blocks away. Steve gazed longingly. He could have used help. But to approach Rawls without tangible proof might be a dangerous mistake. It would, at best, mean long and wordy explanations that would probably not be believed, with almost the certainty that the real quarry would get wind of what was up and would take steps to make sure they were not caught with tangible evidence.

It would be his unsupported word—if he lived long enough, for there was also the probability that he might be shot down before he could make explanation of any kind.

A heavy-shouldered rider appeared in the street, accompanied by a smaller person. Steve stiffened, peering. It was Amos Whipple, and with him was Eileen.

He hugged the shadows, but he had the impression that both she and Amos had picked him out there. However, they moved steadily on down the street and he decided that he had only imagined that they had spotted him.

He peered out. They had already vanished somewhere—into the next cross street evidently.

He again pulled back suddenly. Burl Talley was in sight. He had emerged from the dining room of the Pioneer House. His jaunty, straight figure was unmistakable in the window lights as he came strolling down the street with the air of a man who had just finished a satisfying supper.

Steve edged back and watched Talley move past, puffing a cigar and slapping a pair of riding gloves into a palm. The man was the picture of a person with only business matters on his mind as he walked across the street and entered the office of his lumber business.

Steve swiftly left his covert, crossed the thoroughfare also, and stood at the corner of the office, just off Bozeman Street. The open window was almost above him.

He heard Creed say in a strained, angry voice, "You took your damned time about it. We've been coolin'——"

"Shut up!" Talley's lowered voice was thin and savage. "You fool! If I was to start scurrying around, somebody might . . ."

Talley came to the window and lowered the sash as he talked, and from then on all that Steve heard was a drift of unintelligible talk that was obviously bitter.

Some agreement evidently was finally reached. The glow of light faded. One of the lamps had been snuffed and the wick of the other turned down to leave a faint night light.

Steve heard the two leave by a rear door which opened directly into the lumberyard. He moved into the street toward the wagon gate with the thought in mind that he would slide over it into the enclosure. But he halted after one step, then inched back out of sight into his original position around the corner of the office structure. A man's head was visible above the closed gate. Someone was standing there on lookout.

Steve held his breath for seconds, then relaxed as he became certain that he had not been seen.

He waited. He was sure that feverish activity was under way somewhere around the planing mill in the depths of the property. But the sibilant sounds he picked up had no meaning.

Suddenly the wagon gate was swung open and two mounted men rode into the street. They jogged at a leisurely pace up the thoroughfare in the direction of the road to the upper basin. They were Tex Creed and the mill boss, Whitey Bird.

The stamp of idle hooves sounded faintly inside the lumberyard. Five minutes passed. Ten. Saddle rigging creaked as someone mounted. A voice spoke a command, along with the slap of a rope-end on hide. Breeching groaned and High-river came riding out of the lumberyard leading two horses bearing packsaddles on which were lashed full sacks of grain, three on each load.

Highriver also headed up Bozeman Street, moving without haste. To all appearances he was bound for the Rafter O with grain for the remuda. The two pack animals bore the Rafter O iron and Steve realized that these animals and the saddle horse Whitey Bird had been riding, were the ones Creed and Highriver had brought down from winter range during the day. Evidently the horses had been shifted into town and to the lumberyard after dark.

Steve recrossed the street in a hurry to where his horse waited in the side street. He placed a foot in the stirrup and started to rise into the saddle.

Not until then did he know that two other riders were waiting nearby in the shadows. One moved in alongside of him. His six-shooter came swiftly into his hand, but it was Eileen's voice that halted him. "Steve!"

The bigger figure was that of Amos Whipple.

"I rode to Center Fire and found Uncle Amos," Eileen said. "I told him everything. I knew you'd need help. We came to town as fast as we could make it. We spotted you watching Talley's office but were afraid to make ourselves known for fear we might spoil things. We circled the block and located your horse and waited."

Steve still waited, gazing grimly and inquiringly at Amos.

"Eileen didn't quite tell me everything," Amos said. "She only told me I was a pigheaded, blind, opinionated fool who wanted to go around and hang people on mere suspicion. She said you wasn't a train robber, but that you were being forced to try, lone-handed, to run down the real gang. But she hadn't told me anything I hadn't already learned earlier."

"Already learned?"

Amos nodded. "Douglas had told me everything before Eileen showed up. I didn't know he was in his room. His mother kept it quiet. But when he got on his feet he came down an' faced me. He called me about the same things Eileen did. He was referrin' to my leadin' the Vigilantes an'——"

Steve stopped him with a gesture. "Later!" he said. "They're pulling out and I think they've got the money."

He looked at Eileen and said, "Stay in the clear."

He mounted and headed down the back street, circling four blocks before turning back into Bozeman Street. He discovered that Amos was at his heels.

"Do you really want to get into this, Amos?" he asked. "There's going to be gunplay."

"Never wanted anything so much in my life," Amos said. "Maybe I can sort of make up for a lot of things."

They entered Bozeman Street. The lighted jail office stood directly toward their right, and advancing toward them was Highriver and the two loaded packhorses.

Steve chose this spot to challenge the man. He pulled up his horse in midstreet and sat there as Highriver came riding closer. His quarry rose in the stirrups, peering through the darkness, trying to make out who he was.

Realization came to Highriver. He swung a quirt, lashing at the slow-footed packhorses, sending them into a startled surge ahead. It was a futile thing—the action of one whose mind had been stampeded.

Steve pulled his horse out of the way of the lurching animals. "Don't try to make a fight of it, Highriver," he said.

Highriver was carrying a brace of pistols. He drew and fired. Steve also fired, but his horse was rearing, startled by the violence of his movement and neither his nor Highriver's bullets found their mark.

Steve's mount began buck-jumping. He left the saddle, landing off balance, but still on his feet. A bullet tore his hat from his head. Highriver's six-shooters were blazing at him. It did not seem possible the man could continue to miss him at that close range.

Then Highriver's pistols went silent and he seemed to be impaled on some agonizing force. He rose numbly in the saddle, dropping his guns and clutching at his side. He collapsed abruptly and pitched limply into the street.

Steve realized that it was Amos who had fired the shot that had halted the man.

Eileen's voice screamed, "Behind you, Steve! Uncle Amos!"

Steve pivoted. Tex Creed and Whitey Bird, mounted, were riding into the street and bearing down on them. They had evidently been waiting on the fringe of town to join Highriver, and the gun fight had brought them back.

Creed was shooting. Amos said something in a shocked voice and reeled in the saddle. His right arm, which was his shooting arm, had been broken by one of Creed's bullets.

Marshal Mart Lowery was the first man to emerge from the jail office. He had a .45 in his hand and he was shouting, "Stop it! Stop it!"

Whitey Bird shot the marshal through the body. Lowery pitched backwards into the jail office, falling against Sheriff Bill Rawls who was coming at a run. Rawls eased his fall and rushed onto the sidewalk, a gun in his hand. He crouched there confused, trying to decide his target.

Steve and Creed shot at each other. Steve fired again. The bullet struck Creed in the shoulder, whirling him around. His weight upset the horse, which was rearing, and both animal and rider went down. Creed was thrown clear and lay there on his face. The horse arose and rabbit-jumped down the street, trying to buck off the saddle.

Steve veered his gun upon Whitey Bird, but held his fire. The powdersmoke from a shot, which had centered on the man, was spinning in a ring in the beam of light from the jail office. Mart Lowery, with blood flowing from the wound Bird had given him, had pulled himself up on his elbows and had fired back. Bird clung to the saddlehorn a moment, and then fell to the ground.

Silence came. Rawls, who had not used his .45, still stood on the sidewalk, bewildered. He kept repeating the command Mart Lowery had used. "Stop it! Stop it, in the name of the law!"

Across the street and not a score of yards away was Nick Latzo's Blue Moon. The swing doors had parted and Latzo himself had emerged. He stood there an instant, staring at the scene in the street. Then he understood!

He tried to turn and dart back into the shelter of his gambling house. But Steve said, "No, Nick!"

Latzo halted, gazing at him. "All right," Steve said. "You killed Buck Santee, Nick. Lift your hands."

Latzo was not one to surrender. "To hell with you!" he said in his heavy voice.

He drew and fired. And missed. He fired again. And again he missed.

Steve killed him. He shot Latzo twice and both bullets tore through the man's chest. Latzo lived long enough to try to fire again and did succeed in exploding one wild shot before he collapsed on the threshold of his gambling house.

Steve caught up the hackamore ropes of the pack horses, which were pitching wildly, terrorized by the gunfire. He soothed them with his voice, and they quieted.

"Good Jupiter, Santee!" Rawls began in a stunned voice. "What——?"

"A knife," Steve said. "I want your pocketknife."

Numbly Rawls produced one. Steve opened a blade and slit one of the bulging grain sacks on a packsaddle. Oats streamed into the street at his feet.

But in the split bag was something else that did not yield. Steve reached in and pulled. Smaller canvas bags which contained the hard weight of metal began dropping from the larger container. Gold coin!

He looked at Rawls and at excited citizens who were arriving. "There's your train robbery money," he said. "Part of it, at least. From all three holdups, most likely. This is the share belonging to Creed, Highriver, and Whitey Bird. They were afraid the game had played out, and forced their boss to hand over their share of the loot. They intended to be long gone from the Powderhorn before morning. You'll find the rest of their money in those other grain sacks."

"How——?" Rawls began.

"I believe I know how they vanished without leaving a trail after the Three Forks holdup," Steve said. "They probably had a wagonload of lumber waiting at some trail which crossed the railroad. They pulled the express car alongside, hid the gold and themselves among the lumber, then let the engine and car drift farther along the line. Whitey Bird drove the wagon right into town and into Talley's lumberyard bold as brass."

Steve turned and began running down Bozeman Street toward the lumberyard.

"Don't!" Eileen screamed. "Wait!"

Steve kept going. He was still a block from the dark establishment when a rider came spurring from the gate.

It was Talley. It had taken the man those few minutes since the gun fight had started in the street to saddle a horse and make his bid to escape.

He saw Steve racing toward him and fired a hasty shot which went wide. He used a spur on his mount. The horse was a powerful, well-bred sorrel. With darkness to help him Talley might have had better than an even chance of escaping if he could have got clear of town.

But a new rider appeared in the street ahead of him,

149

blocking his path. It was Doug Whipple. He was hatless and pale and wore only a duck saddle-jacket over the bandage that his mother had wound around his body.

"Pull up, Burl!" Doug said. "We'll face the music together."

Talley lifted his gun and fired. Steve heard the impact of the bullet. Doug was lifted from the saddle. He landed heavily in the street, rolled over, and pulled himself tenaciously to an elbow and shot the horse Talley was riding.

The animal broke in stride and pitched forward in a somersault, breaking its neck. Talley was thrown onto the sidewalk, where he crashed against a water barrel. He lay dazed.

Doug sank down like a man utterly spent after a long race. Steve got to his side and lifted his head.

Doug looked up at him and said in a voice that drifted off, "I heard Eileen when she came to the ranch to get Dad. I followed. It's better this way, Steve."

He said nothing more. A few moments later he was dead.

Steve did not move for a time. Eileen arrived. She knelt beside him and took one of Doug's hands, holding it against her. She began to weep.

Burl Talley was reviving. Steve slowly lowered Doug's head, arose, and walked to Talley. He placed a boot hard on the man's back, pinning him down.

"All we need to know from you, Burl," he said, "is where the rest of the money is cached in your lumberyard. That would be your share. And probably Nick Latzo's."

Sheriff Rawls came lumbering up, panting. "Not you, Burl?" he said. "Not you, of all people?"

"Him, of all people," Steve said. "He's all yours, Rawls."

Eileen arose from Doug's side. Tears stained her cheeks, but she had a grip on herself. "Are you hurt?" she asked Steve.

He decided that he had escaped unharmed, but she drew him into the light to make sure. All she could find was a bullet burn on his left wrist. She drooped a little then, all the strain and sadness hitting her.

He placed an arm around her and they walked back to the jail. Whitey Bird was dead, along with Nick Latzo. Creed and Highriver were alive and would probably pull through, the doctor said. Also Mart Lowery.

A doctor was working on Amos Whipple's arm in the sheriff's office.

Amos looked at Steve and Eileen and Rawls when they entered. "Douglas is dead, ain't he?" he asked dully.

Steve nodded. Amos drew a tired sigh. "What am I ever goin' to tell his mother?" he asked helplessly.

When he was better able to talk, Amos related the whole story to Rawls, with Steve filling in the details in the matter of Frank Clum and Nick Latzo's part in the death of Buck Santee. Amos did not withhold anything in telling of his son's confession to taking part in the two train robberies.

"I guess Douglas came here tonight to pay for what he'd done," he concluded. "And he paid."

He looked at Steve. "I'd give a lot if I could make up for what I did to your father," he said. "But I can't. You can't ever go back—not after they've died to show that you were wrong."

Burl Talley, handcuffed to deputies, was brought in. They had found his pockets stuffed with banknotes, which, no doubt, was a part of the loot from the robberies.

Talley looked at Eileen and some of his jauntiness returned. "I'd have been a rich man if things had worked out my way, Eileen," he said. "And you'd have worn diamonds and sables."

She shook her head. "You don't know people, Burl," she said. "You always were wrong about important things."

Talley was taken away to a cell. He was refusing to talk, demanding a lawyer. But Highriver and Creed, hoping for leniency from the law, were making a clean breast of events.

Steve turned to leave the office. Rawls halted him. "I know where you're going," he said. "To the Silver Moon. Louie Latzo."

"Yes," Steve said. "He'll talk."

"We'll see to it that he talks," Rawls said. "But this is for the law." He glanced toward Eileen. "You don't owe it to her to get yourself killed, now that you've gone this far. Louie won't get away. That's a promise. I'll ask him about Clum's murder. And your father's."

Rawls and his deputies were gone less than an hour. They brought Louie Latzo back with them in handcuffs. By that time the remainder of the train robbery money had been recovered from the sawdust pit at Burl Talley's planing mill, where Creed and Highriver had told them to look.

Rawls nodded at Steve. "Louie talked, with a little persuasion. It was Nick who ambushed your Dad and Henry Thane three years ago. I don't like to have to tell you this, but Buck Santee's body was dropped in an old prospect shaft in the hills, and the shaft was closed with a stick of dynamite."

Steve said nothing. Eileen's fingers squeezed his arm comfortingly.

"An' we won't ever be able to recover Choctaw's body either, I'm afraid," Rawls said. "According to Louie it was Al Painter an' Varney, who were sent out to move him from your saddle shed that night. They sunk Choctaw in an alkali bog way out in the east flats. They set fire to your house too. Varney an' Painter skipped out while we were grabbing Louie, but we'll round 'em up sooner or later."

Doug's body had been placed on a stretcher in the side room at the jail. Steve entered this room, pulled back the sheet, and stood looking down for a time. Doug seemed serene enough in his long sleep.

Steve replaced the sheet and turned away. He and Eileen walked out of the sheriff's office and stood in the cool night air.

"Where do you want to go?" she asked.

"Home, Eileen," he said.

"That will be Antler," she said. "Antler and the OK will be home for both of us now."

He drew her into his arms, and she clung tightly to him for a moment. She kissed him.

And a few minutes later they rode out of Bugle side by side.

Cliff Farrell was born in Zanesville, Ohio, where earlier Zane Grey had been born. Following graduation from high school, Farrell became a newspaper reporter. Over the next decade he worked his way west by means of a string of newspaper jobs and for thirty-one years was employed, mostly as sports editor, for the *Los Angeles Examiner*. He would later claim that he began writing for pulp magazines because he grew bored with journalism. His first Western stories were written for *Cowboy Stories* in 1926 and his byline was A. Clifford Farrell. By 1928 this byline was abbreviated to Cliff Farrell, and this it remained for the rest of his career. In 1933 Farrell was invited to contribute a story for the first issue of *Dime Western*. He soon became a regular contributor to this magazine and to *Star Western* as well. In fact, many months he would have a short novel in both magazines. Farrell became such a staple at Popular Publications that by the end of the 1930s he was contributing as much as 400,000 words a year to their various Western magazines. In all, Farrell wrote nearly 600 stories for the magazine market. His earliest Western fiction tended to stress action and gun play, but increasingly his stories began to focus on characters in historical situations and the problems faced by those characters. *Follow the New Grass* (1954) was Farrell's first Western novel, a story concerned with a desperate battle over grazing rights in the Cheyenne Indian reserve. It was followed by *West with the Missouri* (1955), an exciting story of riverboats, gamblers, and gunmen. *Fort Deception* (1960), *Ride the Wild Country* (1963), *The Renegade* (1970), and *The Devil's Playground* (1976) are among the best of Farrell's later Western novels. *Desperate Journey*, a first collection of Cliff Farrell's Western short stories, has also been published.